Y0-FKW-473

CATWOMAN

VOL. 2 CAT INTERNATIONAL

CATWOMAN

VOL. 2 CAT INTERNATIONAL

TINI HOWARD
WRITER

NICO LEON
SAMI BASRI WITH
VICENTE CIFUENTES
CAITLIN YARSKY
INAKI MIRANDA
JUAN FERREYRA
ROBBI RODRIGUEZ
ARTISTS

VERONICA GANDINI
JORDIE BELLAIRE
JUAN FERREYRA
LEE LOUGHRIDGE
COLORISTS

TOM NAPOLITANO
LUCAS GATTONI
JOSH REED
DERON BENNETT
LETTERERS

JEFF DÉKAL
COLLECTION
COVER ARTIST

JESSICA CHEN
Editor - Original Series
& Collected Edition

JESSICA BERBEY
Assistant Editor - Original Series
& Collected Edition

STEVE COOK
Design Director - Books
& Publication Design

SUZANNAH ROWNTREE
Publication Production

MARIE JAVINS
Editor-in-Chief, DC Comics

ANNE DePIES
Senior VP - General Manager

JIM LEE
Publisher & Chief Creative Officer

DON FALLETTI
VP - Manufacturing Operations & Workflow Management

LAWRENCE GANEM
VP - Talent Services

ALISON GILL
Senior VP - Manufacturing & Operations

JEFFREY KAUFMAN
VP - Editorial Strategy & Programming

NICK J. NAPOLITANO
VP - Manufacturing Administration & Design

NANCY SPEARS
VP - Revenue

CATWOMAN VOL. 2: CAT INTERNATIONAL

Published by DC Comics. Compilation and all new material Copyright © 2023 DC Comics. All Rights Reserved. Originally published in single magazine form in *Catwoman* 45-50. Copyright © 2022 DC Comics. All Rights Reserved. All characters, their distinctive likenesses, and related elements featured in this publication are trademarks of DC Comics. The stories, characters, and incidents featured in this publication are entirely fictional. DC Comics does not read or accept unsolicited submissions of ideas, stories, or artwork.

DC Comics, 4000 Warner Blvd., Bldg. 700, 2nd Floor, Burbank, CA 91522
Printed by Solisco Printers, Scott, QC, Canada. 3/17/23. First Printing.
ISBN: 978-1-77952-032-6

Library of Congress Cataloging-in-Publication Data is available.

PEFC Certified
This product is from sustainably managed forests and controlled sources
PEFC/26-31-02
www.pefc.org

CATWOMAN #45
1:25 VARIANT COVER
BY SOZOMAIKA

DARIO'S CAMERAS AW MOVEMENT AT THE CKS, BUT EIKO AND THE ASIGAWA CLAN DON'T AVE ANY DELIVERIES ON HEIR SCHEDULE. WHICH MEANS IT SHOULDN'T BE HAPPENING.
YOU'LL WANT ME AS BACKUP. HAPPY TO HELP.
ARE YOU AND EIKO... GETTING ALONG?
I TRUST THE WAY EIKO RUNS THE DOCKS, YAKUZA OR OTHERWISE. BUT IF I'M EXPECTING HER KOBUN TO BE MY BACKUP AND THEY'RE NOT THERE...
CATWOMAN
TINI HOWARD STORY
SAMI BASRI PENCILS
VICENTE CIFUENTES INKS
ROBBI RODRIGUEZ ART (PP 12-14)
JORDIE BELLAIRE COLORS
TOM NAPOLITANO LETTERS
JEFF DÉKAL COVER
JENNY FRISON VARIANT COVER
SOZOMAIKA 1:25 VARIANT COVER
JESSICA BERBEY ASSISTANT EDITOR
JESSICA CHEN EDITOR
BEN ABERNATHY GROUP EDITOR
WHAT'S THAT OLD SAYING? WE'RE... THICK AS THIEVES.
IN GENERAL, I'D PREFER TO KEEP HER AND THE REST OF THE MOBSTERS MANAGED. LET THEM HANDLE IT UNDER MY EYE, WHERE I CAN SEE, AND I'LL BE A BUFFER BETWEEN THEM AND THE BAT.
GOTHAM CITY. NOW.
ARE...YOU AND HIM GETTING ALONG?
...WE HAVE A STRICT NON-AGGRESSION PACT.
PARK THE BIKE AND MEET ME UP TOP.
...
...YOU'LL HAVE TO LET GO, VALMONT.
ONE THOUSAND PARDONS.

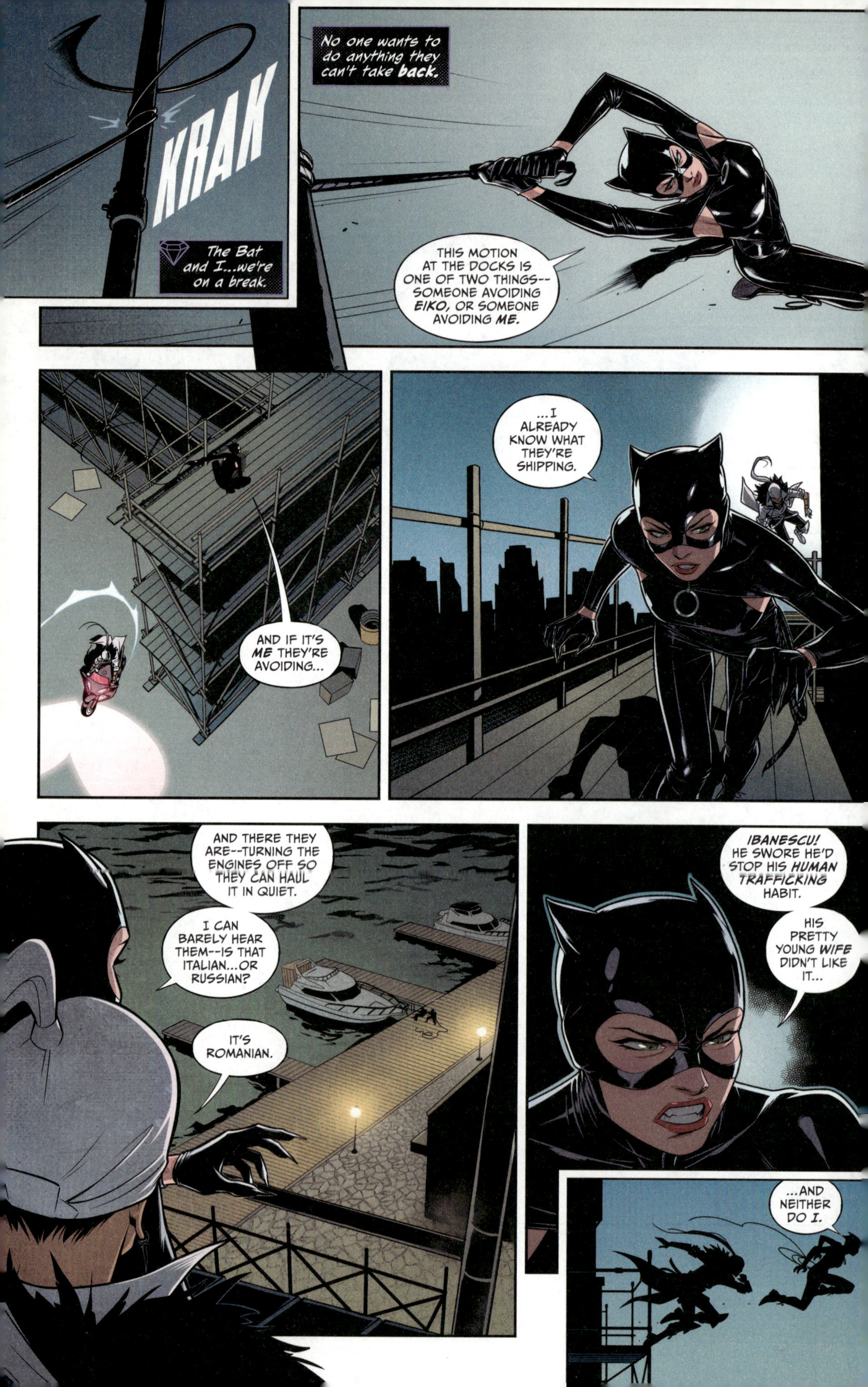
KRAK
The Bat and I...we're on a break.
No one wants to do anything they can't take back.
THIS MOTION AT THE DOCKS IS ONE OF TWO THINGS--SOMEONE AVOIDING EIKO, OR SOMEONE AVOIDING ME.
AND IF IT'S ME THEY'RE AVOIDING...
...I ALREADY KNOW WHAT THEY'RE SHIPPING.
AND THERE THEY ARE--TURNING THE ENGINES OFF SO THEY CAN HAUL IT IN QUIET.
I CAN BARELY HEAR THEM--IS THAT ITALIAN...OR RUSSIAN?
IT'S ROMANIAN.
IBANESCU! HE SWORE HE'D STOP HIS HUMAN TRAFFICKING HABIT.
HIS PRETTY YOUNG WIFE DIDN'T LIKE IT...
...AND NEITHER DO I.

LISA, RIGHT?
MY NAME'S DIONNE. WE'RE GONNA BE OKAY--
...
MMMF!
AAH!
<--SHUT UP IN THERE!>
<YOU BE QUIET. PAINTINGS OF PRETTY WOMEN DON'T TALK, HAHA.>
<HEH. BUT THE REAL THING CAN DO A LOT OF THINGS THE PAINTING CAN'T, YES?>
THOK
HHK!

--YOU'RE RIGHT ABOUT THAT.
YOU PIGS BETTER GET THE #@$% OFF THIS DOCK, OR WE'LL SMEAR YOU ON THIS PAVEMENT, GOD HELP ME!
PISICI! IT'S THAT CRAZY @#$%#~% CAT!
AAAHH!
KRSSHHHH

NO--
KRAK
HRGG--
YOU SNEAK WOMEN INTO MY CITY LIKE PROPERTY?!
I WANT TO MAKE SURE I NEVER FORGET A FACE LIKE YOURS.
SLASHH
AAAAH!
SAY THE WORD, CATWOMAN, AND HE'S NOTHING.
NO.
KNOCK HIM OUT OR SOMETHING, THESE WOMEN NEED US.
AS YOU WISH.
bonk
ARE YOU TWO OKAY? I'M CATWOMAN, AND I WANT TO HELP. IF YOU'LL LET ME.
YOU'VE GOT TO GET OFF THIS DOCK, BUT I'LL HELP YOU GET WHEREVER YOU WANT TO GO-- METROPOLIS, CANCUN, QURAC.
WHAT'S QURAC?
I WANT TO GO HOME.

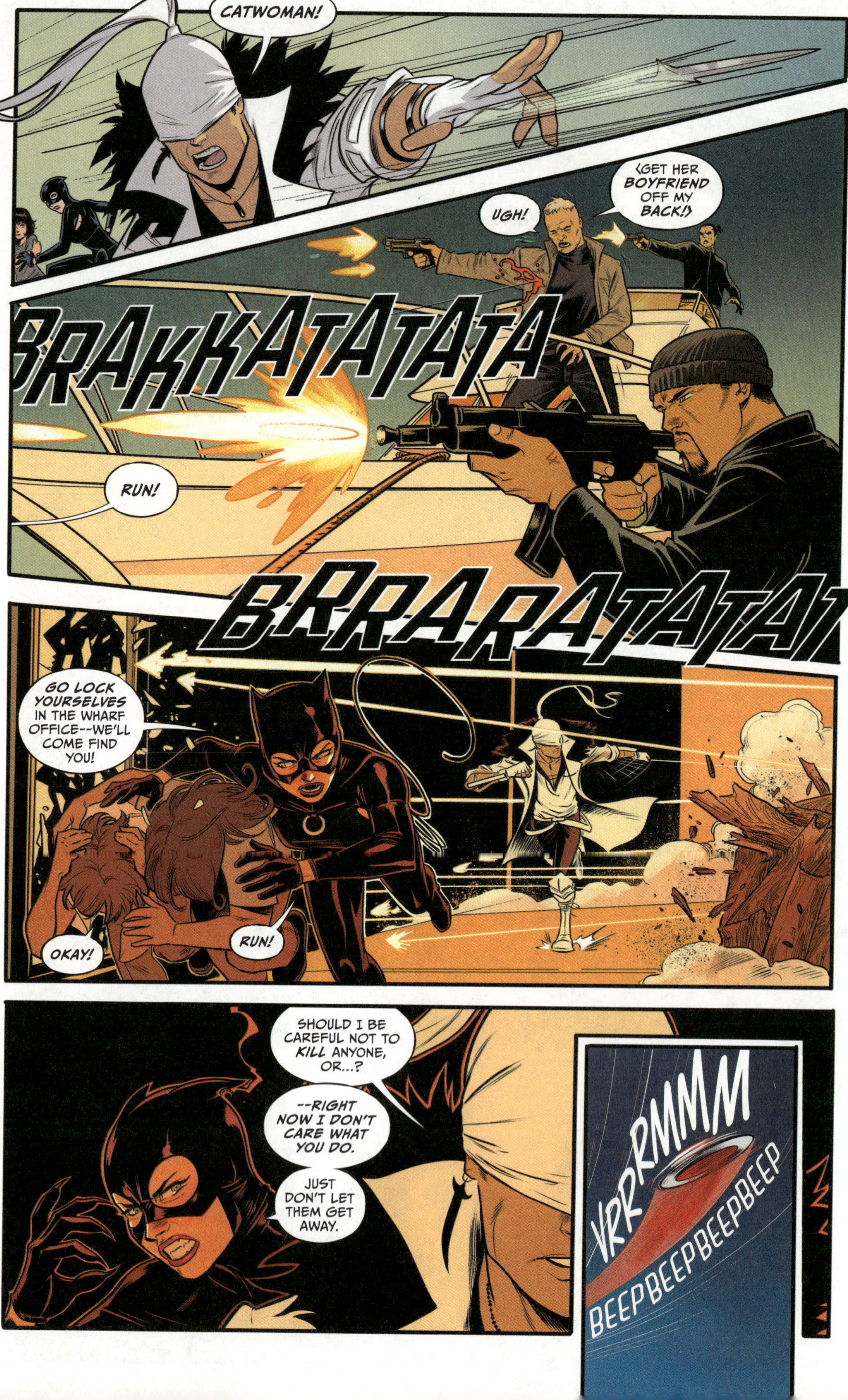
CATWOMAN!
UGH!
‹GET HER BOYFRIEND OFF MY BACK!›
BRAKKATATATA
RUN!
BRRRARATATAT
GO LOCK YOURSELVES IN THE WHARF OFFICE--WE'LL COME FIND YOU!
OKAY!
RUN!
SHOULD I BE CAREFUL NOT TO KILL ANYONE, OR...?
--RIGHT NOW I DON'T CARE WHAT YOU DO.
JUST DON'T LET THEM GET AWAY.
VRRRMMM
BEEPBEEPBEEPBEEP

thunk
KABOOOOM
IT'S THE YAKUZA!
NO WAY--I CAN HEAR THEIR BIKES A MILE AWAY--
I NEED A BETTER LINE OF SIGHT--
IS THAT NOT A MOTORCYCLE I HEAR NOW?
IT'S NOT ONE OF THEIRS--
SON OF A BAT.
...I KNOW THAT BIKE.

HELLO, ROBIN.
AUUGH! CATWOMAN! IS THAT YOU?!
YOU'RE GONNA KILL US BOTH!
WHAT ARE YOU DOING?
GETTING AN EXPLANATION.
THAT'S A FINE WAY TO TALK TO THE PERSON WHO CLEANED UP THESE DOCKS WHILE YOU WERE AWAY AND CAME BACK JUST IN TIME TO SAVE YOUR TAIL!
SKREEE
YOU DID WHAT?
...THIS PLACE WAS CRAWLING WITH YAKUZA.
WHEN I SAW YOU THERE TONIGHT, I'D HOPED YOU'D FOLLOW ME AND WE'D REGROUP, SEE WHAT WE CAN DO ABOUT THAT BOAT, AND THEN--

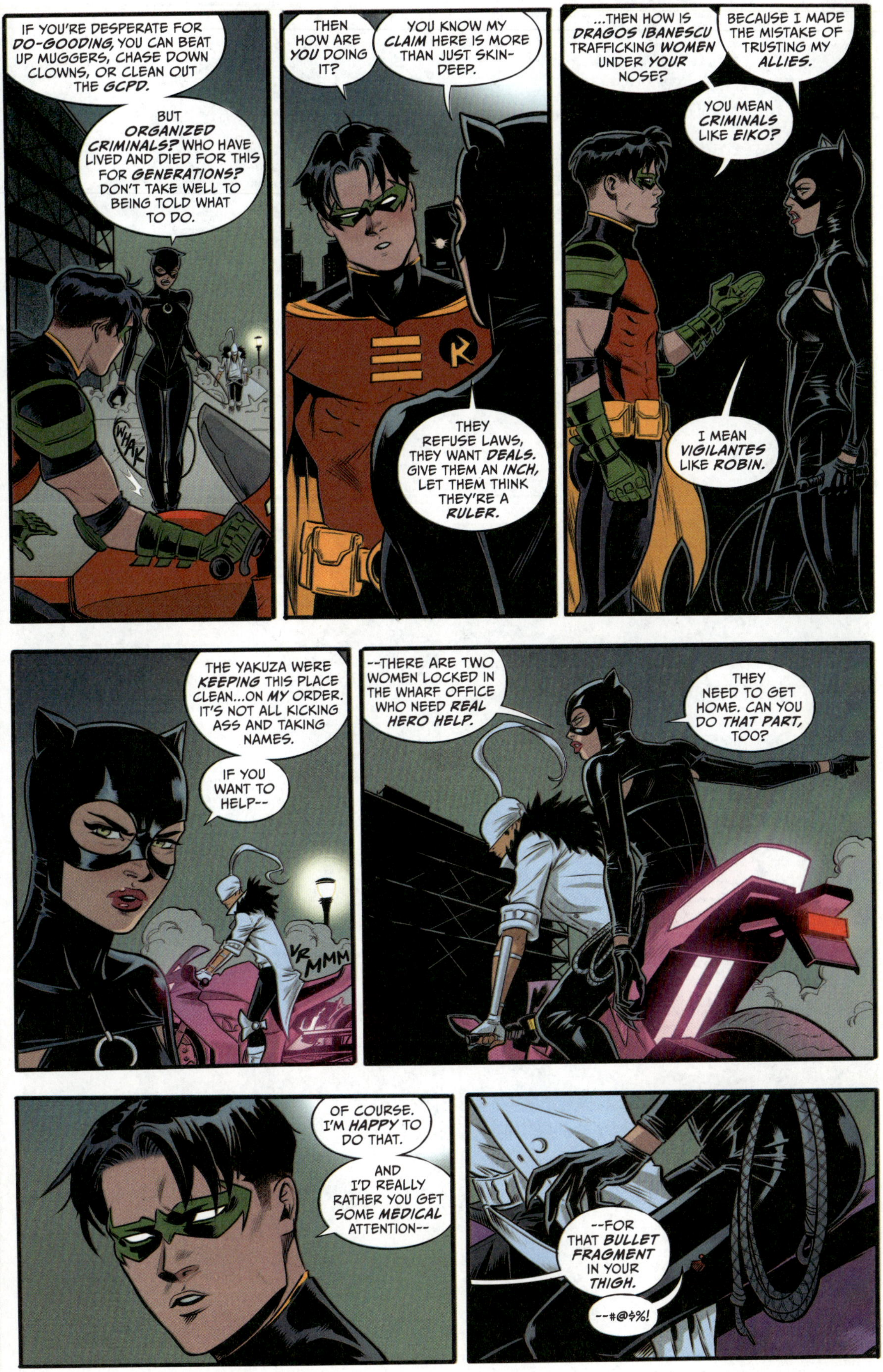
IF YOU'RE DESPERATE FOR DO-GOODING, YOU CAN BEAT UP MUGGERS, CHASE DOWN CLOWNS, OR CLEAN OUT THE GCPD.
BUT ORGANIZED CRIMINALS? WHO HAVE LIVED AND DIED FOR THIS FOR GENERATIONS? DON'T TAKE WELL TO BEING TOLD WHAT TO DO.
WHAK
THEN HOW ARE YOU DOING IT?
YOU KNOW MY CLAIM HERE IS MORE THAN JUST SKIN-DEEP.
THEY REFUSE LAWS, THEY WANT DEALS. GIVE THEM AN INCH, LET THEM THINK THEY'RE A RULER.
...THEN HOW IS DRAGOS IBANESCU TRAFFICKING WOMEN UNDER YOUR NOSE?
BECAUSE I MADE THE MISTAKE OF TRUSTING MY ALLIES.
YOU MEAN CRIMINALS LIKE EIKO?
I MEAN VIGILANTES LIKE ROBIN.
THE YAKUZA WERE KEEPING THIS PLACE CLEAN...ON MY ORDER. IT'S NOT ALL KICKING ASS AND TAKING NAMES.
IF YOU WANT TO HELP--
VRMMM
--THERE ARE TWO WOMEN LOCKED IN THE WHARF OFFICE WHO NEED REAL HERO HELP.
THEY NEED TO GET HOME. CAN YOU DO THAT PART, TOO?
OF COURSE. I'M HAPPY TO DO THAT.
AND I'D REALLY RATHER YOU GET SOME MEDICAL ATTENTION--
--FOR THAT BULLET FRAGMENT IN YOUR THIGH.
--#@$%!

LATER...
YOU WOULDN'T BELIEVE HOW MANY APARTMENTS IN THIS CITY ARE DISUSED LEAGUE OF ASSASSINS SAFE HOUSES.
WITH THE WAY GOTHAM'S RENT HAS GONE UP? I SURE WOULD.
LEAGUE'S STILL NOT AS BAD AS THOSE RICH GUYS WHO BUY UP APARTMENTS JUST TO RENT 'EM OUT ONLINE--
--HISHHHH-- OW!
SO SORRY.
THIS WAS NOT A DIRECT HIT, BUT A BULLET THAT RICOCHETED. MUST BE WHY YOU DID NOT NOTICE.
AND THE ADRENALINE, OF COURSE. THE WAY OUR HEARTS RACE.
YOU'D KNOW...
...YOU'RE... A KILLER.
HAHAHAHA.
YES, CATWOMAN! IT IS NOT A BASELESS ACCUSATION. YOUR FRIEND ONYX...
...SHE TOO, IS A KILLER.
...NOT ANYMORE.
VERY WELL THEN. NEITHER AM I!
SNIP
POUR VOUS. I RENOUNCE IT!
HAHAHA, I AM. I AM!
BE SERIOUS.
ZRRBT ZRRBT

SELINA.
...BRUCE?
WHAT'S GOING ON, ARE YOU--
I'M FINE. JUST THINKING ABOUT YOU.
SEE BATMAN #125 FOR THE HE SAID TO THIS SHE SAID...AS THERE ARE TWO SIDES TO EVERY STORY.
WONDERING IF...EVERYTHING IS ALL RIGHT.
I'M GOOD.
KEEPING BUSY, YOU KNOW ME. AND...
...I'M SURE YOU'RE THE SAME? BACK IN GOTHAM...
Say something nice--
FOREVER A FIRE TO PUT OUT.
Oh, well done, Kyle.
I HEARD THE ÜBER-RICH ARE BEING HUNTED.
HOPE YOU'RE WATCHING YOUR BACK.
DON'T TELL ME YOU'RE ORDERING TAKEOUT...
...I JUST MADE COFFEE.
VALMONT, I AM ON THE PHONE!
BRUCE, I NEED TO--
IT'S OKAY.
I'VE GOT TO--
Men are just distracting me...

--so let's ask some Batgirls.
IT'S SO COOL THAT YOU'RE HELPING! I MEAN, I THOUGHT, WHEN YOU SHOWED UP...
...YOU WANTED TO STEAL STUFF.
THANK YOU, CASS, I'M LOVING YOUR HONESTY. KEEP IT UP.
OOP--STAY HERE, GIRLS. THINK I HEARD SOMETHING--
ORACLE?
DID YOU TRAIN YOUR TWO LITTLE BAT-MOPPETS TO DO SHTICK?
BATGIRLS WE DOWN *
MOPPETS?
I LIKE IT.
*SEE BATGIRLS #8 FOR WHY ORACLE'S COMMS IS CUTTING OUT! --JESS C.
ORACLE, YOU'RE CUTTING OUT--I CAN'T HEAR YOU.
THE BATGIRLS ARE POSTED UP, BUT IT LOOKS LIKE ONE OF THOSE SAINTS, ASSISI, IS A BIT OF AN ESCAPE ARTIST.
ONE MOMENT PLEASE.
OH BATGIRLS? COME HERE SO I CAN SHOW YOU SOMETHING.
Thud
HEY CATWOMAN--IS IT TRUE YOU RAN INTO RED CLAW? THAT LEGENDARY MERCENARY?

I DID. AND YOU'D BE SURPRISED-- AFTER TALKING, SHE WAS RATHER COOPERATIVE.
RED CLAW'S A SHE? I KNEW IT!
YOU CAN'T JUST TIE HIS TORSO UNLESS HE'S ANCHORED TO SOMETHING.
TIE HIS FEET, TOO.
I THOUGHT I DID!
THEN DO IT AGAIN.
LISTEN, BATGIRLS. I'M HAPPY TO HELP, BUT YOU KNOW ME--AS MUCH GOODNESS AS THERE IS IN MY HEART, I DON'T WORK FOR FREE.
I'M HERE TO ASK WHAT YOUR BUDDY ROBIN'S BEEN FINDING IN THOSE SHIPPING CONTAINERS.
ROBIN SAID YOU CAUGHT THEM SHIPPING... WOMEN.
I'M PUTTING A STOP TO THAT. BUT IF THE WHOLE BAT-CREW JUST DESCENDS ON THEM, IT'LL BE BAD FOR ALL OF US.
DO YOU TRUST ME TO HANDLE IT, KIDDO?
...SO WHAT DO YOU NEED?
SOME SPECIFIC HELP. LATER, YOU CAN HELP ME BEAT THEIR ASSES, AND HELP THOSE GIRLS WHO WILL NEED A FRIEND LIKE YOU SO BADLY.

...THIS WAY.
OH, IS THIS ABOUT THE THING YOU SAW IN ROBIN'S RECORDS? THE ART STUFF?
DO GO ON. IBANESCU'S BEEN CLAIMING ART INVESTMENTS AS HIS MAIN IMPORT FOR YEARS. BLAMES IT ON HIS WIFE'S EXPENSIVE TASTES.
SEE, THERE--ON THE RECORD. THAT PAINTING NAME--THE THREE GRACES BY INFANTINO CARMINI.
ROBIN WAS ABLE TO GET IBANESCU'S SECURITY RECORDS.
AND HE SHARED THEM WITH YOU? THAT'S NICE.
NOT... EXACTLY.
GOOD GIRLS.
BUT THAT HAPPENS TO BE CASS'S FAVORITE PAINTING IN ALL OF GOTHAM.
SO SHE KNEW HE COULDN'T HAVE BOUGHT IT--IT'S STILL DOWNTOWN. MOVED TO THE BASEMENT--BUT IT'S NOT IN HIS COLLECTION. WE'RE SURE.
THE TIMING IS TOO PERFECT THOUGH--IBANESCU MUST HAVE USED THE MOVE AS A COVER-UP...I SUDDENLY HAVE A DISGUSTING FEELING.
READ ME OFF THE NAMES OF SOME MORE OF THOSE PAINTINGS?
THE MAIDENS AT PLAY, SCANDINIOLI'S WOMEN OF VIRTUE, THE BALLERINAS--
--OH I'M GONNA BE SICK.
JUST WHAT I THOUGHT. HE'S USING THE ART TRANSACTIONS TO COVER THE PRICE OF THE WOMEN.
I'VE GOT SOME INVESTIGATING TO DO TO HANDLE THIS. YOU GIRLS TAKE CARE OF YOURSELVES. YOU EVER NEED ME--
YEAH, YEAH.
--OH, AND BY THE WAY, DON'T LET THAT ASSISI CREEP LEER AT YOU--THERE'S A CAMERA IN HIS HELMET.

LATER...
TURNS OUT POP TOMASSO MET WITH DARIO TONIGHT AT CAPULLO'S.
ARE THEY STILL THERE, DARIO?
NOPE, THAT'S WHERE YOU COME IN.
PRRRRRRR
THEY'RE AT MILK, THAT FANCY CLUB WHERE THE GIRLS DON'T STRIP, THEY JUST POUR YOU LIQUOR ALL NIGHT?
ALREADY ON MY WAY.
WAITAMINUTE.
DAD AND IBANESCU SAW YOU AT THE KITTY KAT CLUB. THEY'LL KNOW WHAT YOU LOOK LIKE.
YOU'D BE SURPRISED WHAT A LITTLE MAKEUP AND AN OUTFIT CHANGE CAN ACCOMPLISH.
YOU'RE COMING BACK HERE TO CHANGE? I DON'T KNOW HOW LONG THEY'LL BE THERE, CAT--
MILK
HIII. LATE FOR MY SHIFT.
MRN.

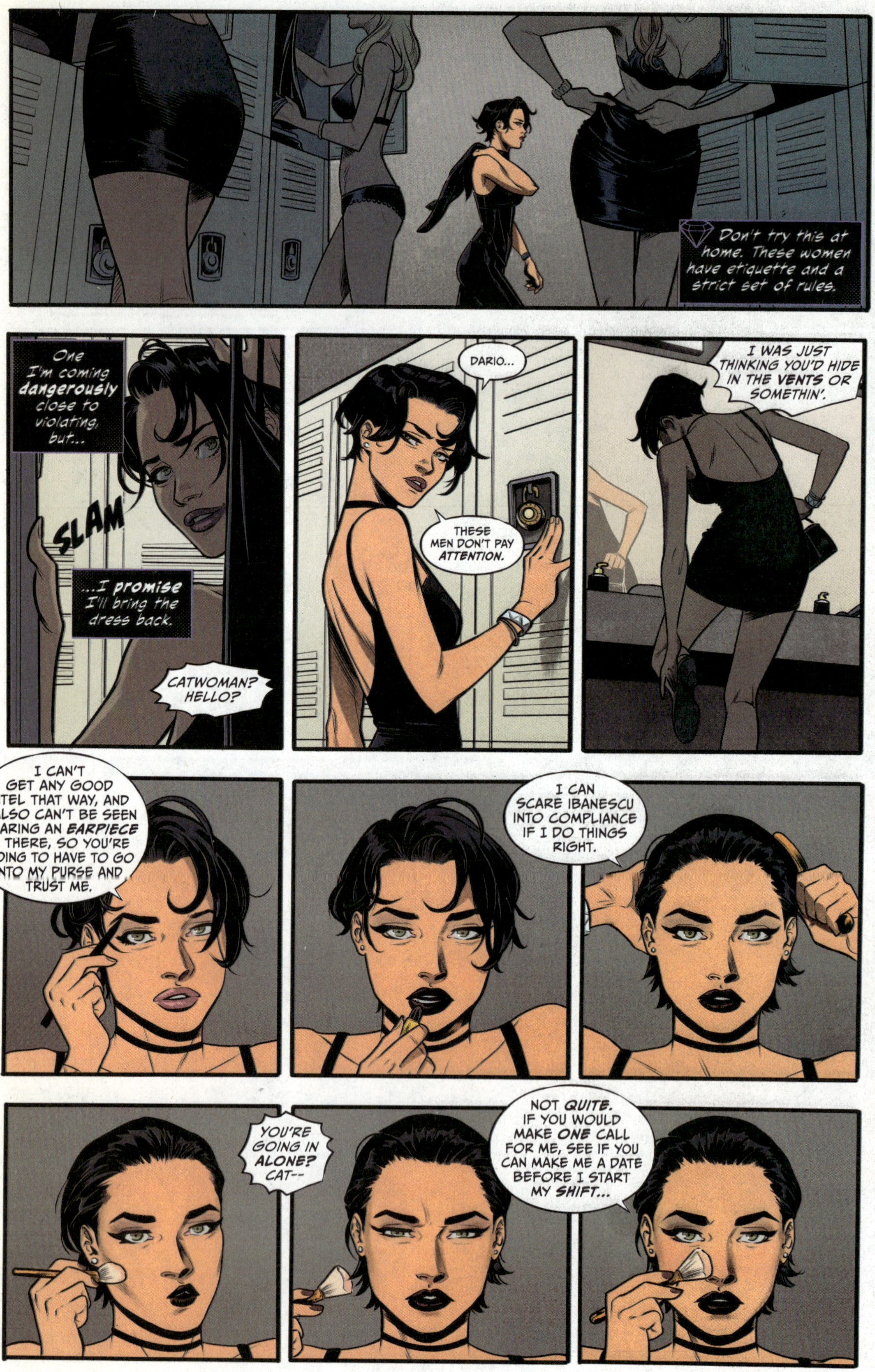
Don't try this at home. These women have etiquette and a strict set of rules.
One I'm coming dangerously close to violating, but...
SLAM
...I promise I'll bring the dress back.
CATWOMAN? HELLO?
DARIO...
THESE MEN DON'T PAY ATTENTION.
I WAS JUST THINKING YOU'D HIDE IN THE VENTS OR SOMETHIN'.
I CAN'T GET ANY GOOD INTEL THAT WAY, AND I ALSO CAN'T BE SEEN WEARING AN EARPIECE IN THERE, SO YOU'RE GOING TO HAVE TO GO INTO MY PURSE AND TRUST ME.
I CAN SCARE IBANESCU INTO COMPLIANCE IF I DO THINGS RIGHT.
YOU'RE GOING IN ALONE? CAT--
NOT QUITE. IF YOU WOULD MAKE ONE CALL FOR ME, SEE IF YOU CAN MAKE ME A DATE BEFORE I START MY SHIFT...

...much to my dismay, I'll need a man on the inside.
YOU KNOW, I HAD MANY GUESSES AS TO HOW YOU WOULD LOOK UNDER THAT MASK.
THOUGH MORE THAN A FEW PATRONS CAN'T STOP TALKING ABOUT YOUR LEGS IN THAT DRESS. CAN'T SAY I BLAME THEM.
SHH. YOU'RE ONLY HERE BECAUSE I NEED AN EXTRA PAIR OF EARS THAT ISN'T ALSO ATTACHED TO A PAIR OF BOOBS.
WHAT WERE THEY MEETING ABOUT? I DON'T DOUBT FOR A SECOND THAT TOMASSO WOULD WANT TO GET INTO THAT DISGUSTING TRAFFICKING GAME.
FROM WHAT I'VE BEEN ABLE TO LIP-READ, THEY HAVEN'T BROUGHT IT UP.
THE HOT TOPIC OF THE EVENING HAS BEEN ROMAN SIONIS.
LEAVING SO SOON?
I'M NOT NEW AT THIS, VALMONT. SWEET-TALKING IS FREE.
SMART GIRLS GO WHERE THE TIPS ARE.

THERE ARE MANY BENEFITS TO THE ARRANGEMENT, I FIND. ROMAN SIMPLY HAS ACCESS TO THINGS THAT WE DO NOT.
I FIND THESE COSTUMED TYPES UNREASONABLE AT BEST...BUT I AM EAGER TO MEET THIS NEW ALLY BLACK MASK IS SO EXCITED ABOUT. I UNDERSTAND HE ARRIVES IN GOTHAM TONIGHT.
HE WOULD CALL SUCH TALK INSULTING.
HAHAHA. TELL ME, IS THE GREAT BLACK MASK STILL HIDING AWAY CRYING BECAUSE HIS SPECIAL MASK GOT BLOWN UP BY CATWOMAN?
ALWAYS A WOMAN'S WAY, TO SMASH YOUR THINGS WHEN THEY ARE MAD.
OF ALL OF THE GIN JOINTS IN GOTHAM CITY--
--IT'S NOT WHAT IT LOOKS LIKE.
DICK GRAYSON. WHAT WOULD BRUCE WAYNE SAY ABOUT YOU SPENDING YOUR MONEY IN A PLACE LIKE THIS?
IF BRUCE GOT A SAY IN WHAT I SPENT MY MONEY ON, HALEY WOULDN'T HAVE SO MANY OUTFITS.
I CAME LOOKING FOR YOU.
YOU CERTAINLY DRESSED LIKE A YOUNG MAN ABOUT TO SEE HIS ALMOST-STEPMOTHER.
DON'T MAKE THIS WEIRD. I WAS ON A DATE WITH BABS.

MUST'VE BEEN A SNOOZE--SHE WAS RUNNING OPS ON THE RADIO WITH ME AND THE BATGIRLS EARLIER TODAY.
FIRST OF ALL--THAT TOOK LIKE FIVE MINUTES. SECOND--GREAT JOB ON THAT HAIR AND MAKEUP, I ALMOST DIDN'T RECOGNIZE YOU.
I NEED TO TELL YOU SOMETHING. ONE OF THE GUYS I KEEP MY EYE ON...HE SEEMS TO BE WORKING FOR ONE OF THE GUYS YOU KEEP AN EYE ON.
WHERE ARE WE GOING?
I'M WORKING. YOU AND YOUR LITTLE BROTHERS CAN QUIT FOLLOWING ME!
WHAT AM I SUPPOSED TO DO IF I THINK YOU'RE IN DANGER? SOCK SOME MONEY AWAY FOR YOUR HOSPITAL BILLS?
THAT WOULD BE VERY KIND, ACTUALLY.
NOW EXCUSE ME WHILE I GO HANDLE HOW BADLY YOU AND YOUR LITTLE FAMILY KEEP COMPROMISING MY WORK.
LOCKER ROOM
BETTER NOT TRY AND FOLLOW ME IN HERE.
THE BOTTLE GIRLS WOULD GET...WAY TOO EXCITED.
SELINA, WAIT.

The kids in Alleytown are too pure. Onyx is **too righteous.** The **Bat-kids** are too noble.
I'm not **changing my mind** about help. I just know what I am. That's why the only people I'll let help me...
...are the ones I'm not scared about bringing down with me.
Sometimes that means I'm all alone.
INCOMING MESSAGE FROM **NIGHTWING.**
...but sometimes even the **bad guys** surprise you with their own loyalty.
VALMONT, WHAT ARE YOU STILL DOING HERE?
I WANTED TO HELP. BUT I DID NOT WANT TO ***CHASE*** YOU, OR DO WHAT THOSE BOYS HAD DONE.
SO I SIMPLY... WAITED.
...WHERE I KNEW YOU COULD FIND ME.

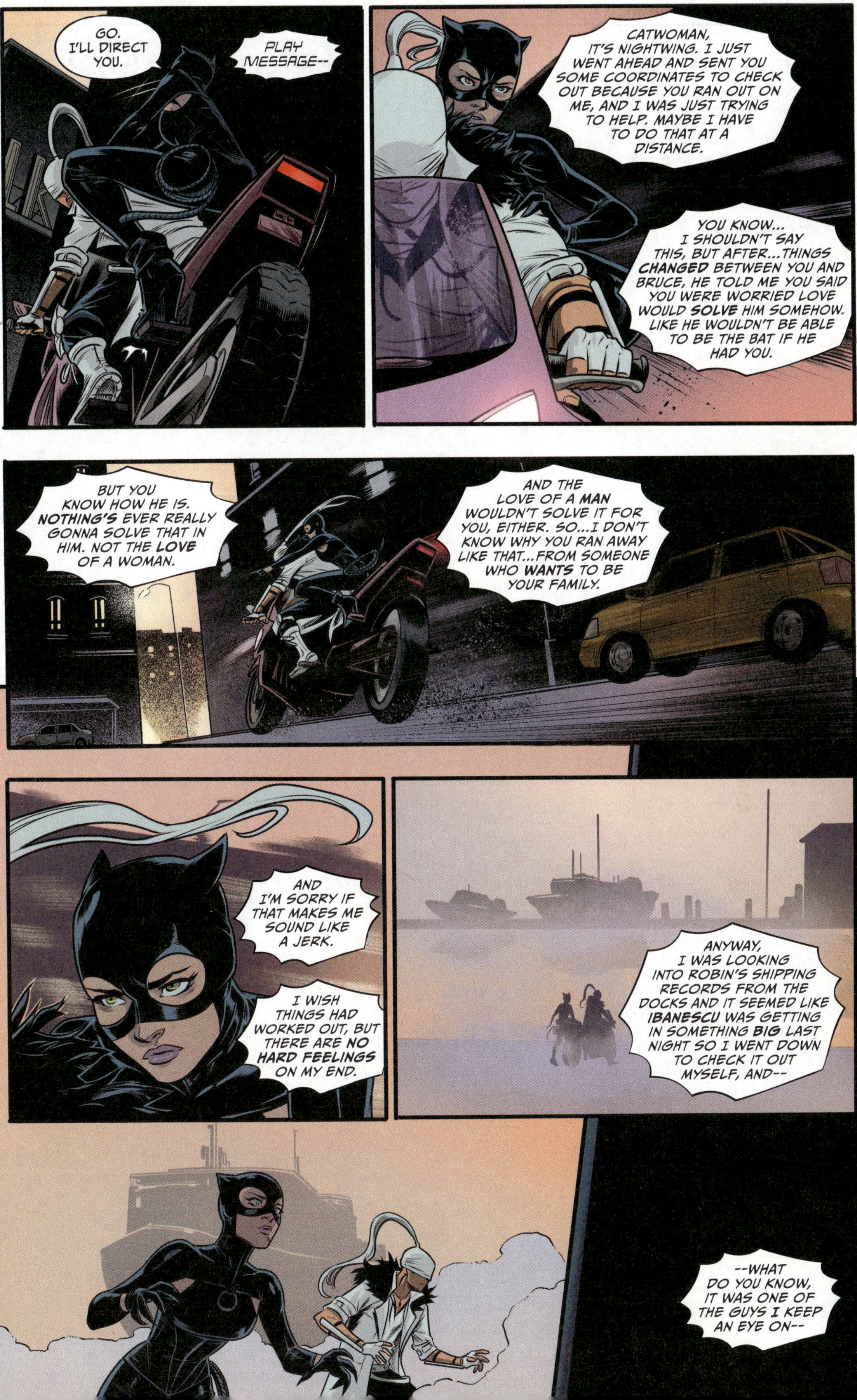
GO. I'LL DIRECT YOU.
PLAY MESSAGE--
CATWOMAN, IT'S NIGHTWING. I JUST WENT AHEAD AND SENT YOU SOME COORDINATES TO CHECK OUT BECAUSE YOU RAN OUT ON ME, AND I WAS JUST TRYING TO HELP. MAYBE I HAVE TO DO THAT AT A DISTANCE.
YOU KNOW... I SHOULDN'T SAY THIS, BUT AFTER...THINGS **CHANGED** BETWEEN YOU AND BRUCE, HE TOLD ME YOU SAID YOU WERE WORRIED LOVE WOULD **SOLVE** HIM SOMEHOW. LIKE HE WOULDN'T BE ABLE TO BE THE BAT IF HE HAD YOU.
BUT YOU KNOW HOW HE IS. **NOTHING'S** EVER REALLY GONNA SOLVE THAT IN HIM. NOT THE **LOVE** OF A WOMAN.
AND THE LOVE OF A **MAN** WOULDN'T SOLVE IT FOR YOU, EITHER. SO...I DON'T KNOW WHY YOU RAN AWAY LIKE THAT...FROM SOMEONE WHO **WANTS** TO BE YOUR FAMILY.
AND I'M SORRY IF THAT MAKES ME SOUND LIKE A JERK.
I WISH THINGS HAD WORKED OUT, BUT THERE ARE **NO HARD FEELINGS** ON MY END.
ANYWAY, I WAS LOOKING INTO ROBIN'S SHIPPING RECORDS FROM THE DOCKS AND IT SEEMED LIKE **IBANESCU** WAS GETTING IN SOMETHING **BIG** LAST NIGHT SO I WENT DOWN TO CHECK IT OUT MYSELF, AND--
--WHAT DO YOU KNOW, IT WAS ONE OF THE GUYS I KEEP AN EYE ON--

--AMYGDALA!
RAAAGH!
ENJOY A DRINK, MY FRIEND!
TO A FANTASTIC NEW COLLABORATION BETWEEN THE MEN OF GOTHAM!
NEXT: SHUT THE CLUB DOWN!

Catwoman #46
1:25 VARIANT COVER BY TULA LOTAY

THEN.
CATWOMAN-- IT ISN'T SAFE HERE. THIS GANG HAS BEEN SUPPLIED FOR WEEKS BY--
MR. FREEZE. THOSE WERE CRYO-ROUNDS.
YOU'RE FAMILIAR?
WEALTHY DOCTOR IN GOTHAM? I KEEP MY EYES ON GUYS LIKE THAT. BESIDES--
I miss him more than you think.
FREEZE'S GUYS HAVE BEEN BIG ABOUT WARNING SHOTS LATELY.
IT'S LIKE THEY DON'T WANT TO GET CAUGHT KILLING FOR HIM--THE PROBLEM WITH USING RENT-A-GOONS.
YES, I'VE NOTED THAT, TOO. VERY ASTUTE.
The good times, sure, of course.

There were so many good times.
More than just this, it was that look he'd get on his face--
...like he was dazzled by me...
ON THE--
LEFT, I SEE HIM. UP TOP!
GOOD EYE.
I liked having someone to team up with. I liked it all.
THIS SHOULD BE THE LAST OF FREEZE'S CELL.
I'LL TAKE IT FROM HERE.
...PURRFECT, LOVER.
I'LL TAKE THIS.
WHAT ARE YOU DOING?
REQUISITIONING THESE MATERIALS.
THEFT IS A CRIME, SELINA.

But sometimes it's this.
CAREFUL, BATMAN, WE'RE IN MASKS.
I'LL PAWN THESE AND MAKE ENOUGH MONEY OR THE ALLEYTOWN 'DS TO GET EASTER BASKETS AND A POOL FOR SUMMER.
SHALL I INSTEAD SURRENDER THESE TO THE GCPD FOR THE CORRUPT COPS TO PLAY WITH?
CAT, I'LL BUY THEM A POOL--
--YOU DON'T NEED TO.
STEALING LIKE THAT IS SHAMELESS. I HAVE MONEY--
This.
I DON'T FEEL A DAMN BIT ASHAMED!
MY ONLY MISTAKE WAS DOING IT WHERE YOU COULD SEE.
This is what I miss most.
It's not every day you meet someone who you love enough to fight with.

Sometimes, I just miss knowing there was someone reliable who had my **back.**
NOW.
VALMONT, WHERE THE HELL ARE YOU?!
KILL KITTY KILL KITTY KILL KITTY! RRAAAAGGHH!!
SMASH
CATWOMAN
TINI HOWARD STORY
SAMI BASRI PENCILS
VICENTE CIFUENTES INKS
JORDIE BELLAIRE COLORS
LUCAS GATTONI LETTERS
JEFF DEKAL COVER
SOZOMAIKA VARIANT COVER
TULA LOTAY 1:25 VARIANT COVER
JEFF DEKAL SWIMSUIT VARIANT COV
JESSICA BERBEY ASSISTANT EDI
JESSICA CHEN EDITOR
BEN ABERNATHY GROUP EDITO

AMYGDALA! I SHOULD HAVE KNOWN SIONIS WOULD ONLY BRING OUT FELLOW LUNATICS!
LET THE MAD BASTARD AT HER! IT WILL BE GOOD FOR HIM...AND FOR US.
COCKY OLD MEN--
--OUT WITHOUT YOUR GUARD UP?
IS THAT TRUE, DON TOMASSO?
GKK-- WE'LL KILL YOU--
YOU'RE WILLING TO KILL FOR DRAGOS IBANESCU?
I DOUBT THAT.
WHAK
SHOVE
THINK IT OVER.
KILL KITTY!

RRRRRAAARRGHHH!!
I SMELL YOU, KITTY!
CRASH
IN WE GO.
breathe
breathe
breathe
C'MON C'MON C'MON...
RRRRR... SNIIIFFF...
THWP

WHAM
WHAM
CATWOMAN?!
WHAM
IBANESCU AND TOMASSO ARE JUST NOW GETTING IN THEIR CARS. WE CAN GET TO THEM--
AND DO WHAT, VALMONT?
MURDER TWO MAFIA DONS IN COLD BLOOD? TAKE THEM TO THE POLICE?
WE CAN'T. THE BIG GUY'S NAPPING. LET'S GET OUT OF HERE.
IS HE...NOT A THREAT?
IT'S COMPLICATED.
HIS REAL NAME'S AARON HELZINGER, AND HE'S A BRAIN INJURY PATIENT, NOT AN EVIL MAN.
I'D FEEL WORSE ABOUT KNOCKING HIM OUT BACK THERE, BUT THE DAMAGE WAS DONE BACK WHEN THEY REMOVED HIS--
AMYGDALA?
EXACTLY.
HE HAS THE CHOICE TO WAKE UP AND REMEMBER THAT MESSING WITH THESE GUYS GETS HIS ASS KICKED.
LET'S HOPE HE DOES.
--?!
AU REVOIR--

SUBTERRANEAN OFFICE OF ROMAN SIONIS, THE BLACK MASK.
GENTLEMEN, LATELY YOU MAY HAVE NOTICED... I'VE HAD A SPATE OF BAD LUCK.
NO KIDDING. CATWOMAN...RED CLAW...EVEN THAT IRRITATING CLAN CHICK, EIKO HASIGAWA.
WHAT DO THEY ALL HAVE IN COMMON?
ROMAN, YOU HAVE LOST YOUR MIND! WHATEVER SENSE YOU HAD LEFT WENT AWAY WHEN CATWOMAN DESTROYED YOUR MASK, WHICH MEANS YOU DIDN'T HAVE MUCH TO BEGIN WITH.
THE ONLY THING I TRUST...
...IS A GENTLEMAN'S WORD. SO I SAY WE CALL THIS... THE GENTLEMAN'S CLUB. WHO DOESN'T LIKE A GENTLEMAN'S CLUB?
DON TOMASSO, DRAGOS IBANESCU, YOUR FIRST MEETING WITH MR. HELZINGER GOT INTERRUPTED BY--YET AGAIN--A NOSY WOMAN WHO UPSET AND ASSAULTED HIM.
YOU CAN FORGIVE THAT, YEAH?

HHHHHH... HLLOOO...
HE'S TRYING.
THIS IS A FUNNY MEETING YOU'VE CALLED, ROMAN. MYSELF AND DRAGOS...BUT NO SIGN OF THE AFOREMENTIONED MISS HASIGAWA, AND MORE CURIOUSLY, NO MR. SULLIVAN.
GUESS I'M SUSPICIOUS BUT I DON'T WANT SOMEONE WHO WANTS TO @#$% CATWOMAN IN OUR COUNCIL OF POWER.
AND FINBAR SULLIVAN IS A DUMB MOOK WHO'S BEEN PUNCHED IN THE HEAD SO MANY TIMES HE'S SCARED OF GIRLS.
PRESENT COMPANY EXCLUDED, MY GUY.
WE ARE ALL A BETTER CLASS OF MAN. WE BACK OUR THREATS WITH DIRECT ACTION, REAL VIOLENCE, NOT THE DECEPTION AND SHADOW WORK OF WOMEN AND THIEVES.
AND WE SURE AS @#$% DON'T NEED TO VOTE ON THINGS.
CAN THE DON BE TRUSTED? LOOK AT DON TOMASSO, FEDERICO, YOUR SON DARIO SHAMES YOU STILL.
WE KNOW HE WILL NOT BED A WOMAN... YET HE SNIFFS AROUND AFTER THE CAT!
I NO LONGER RECOGNIZE A SON, DRAGOS. NOAH GODARD IS MY HEIR.
CRUNCH
TO POWER...
...AND THE SWIFT SEVERANCE OF TIES WITH THOSE WHO WOULD FAIL US.
--TO THE FINEST FELLAS IN GOTHAM.

EIKO HASIGAWA'S YACHT.
THEY THINK I DON'T KNOW THAT THEY'RE MEETING WITHOUT ME.
THEY THINK I'M NOT GOOD ENOUGH TO WORK WITH THEM. THEY'RE FOOLS, THUGS--ON TOP OF THAT, IBANESCU IS A TRAFFICKER OF WOMEN.
FAH, THEY AREN'T GOOD ENOUGH TO WORK FOR ME. FOR MY DOGS.
WHAT HAPPENED TO NOT GIVING UP YOUR HARD-EARNED POWER FOR ME, EIKO?
DON'T FLATTER YOURSELF, SELINA. YOU ARE SIMPLY MORE COMPETENT. BUT DON'T GET ME WRONG.
I'VE ALWAYS FOUND COMPETENCE VERY ATTRACTIVE.
WELL, YOU LOOKED GREAT FOR THAT TIME YOU WORE THE CATSUIT.*
DO YOU STILL HAVE THAT ONE?
*SEE CATWOMAN VOL. 6: THE KEEPER OF THE CASTLE (2014) --JESS C.
I DO.
...SELINA... MAY I BE FORWARD?
PLEASE DON'T SPARE MY FEELINGS ON MATTERS OF STRATEGY.
IT ISN'T BUSINESS. IT'S PERSONAL.

YOU ARE TRYING TO BE A LEADER OF ORGANIZED CRIME, A WORLD BASED ON ABSOLUTE OBEDIENCE, ON WORDS AND VOWS.
BUT YOU ARE EVASIVE, PROUDLY SO. IN THE HASIGAWA CLAN, THINGS ARE BLACK OR WHITE, BUT YOU KNOW WHAT THEY SAY...AT NIGHT, ALL CATS ARE--
--GRAY. WHAT IS THIS ABOUT?
...I HELD OFF FROM PURSUING YOU BECAUSE I THOUGHT YOU WERE STILL...ENTANGLED WITH ANOTHER.
IT'S COMPLICATED...
I'M SURE IT IS, FOR YOU. BUT IT SHOULDN'T HAVE TO BE FOR ME.
IS YOUR HEART OPEN OR NOT, SELINA?
NOT... NOT TO PEOPLE I SO DESPERATELY NEED AS ALLIES. LIKE YOU... AND LIKE... HIM.
SO THEN WHO IS VALMONT TO YOU, SELINA?
HE'S-- ALSO JUST AN ALLY. HE CAME TO THE CITY... HE SAID FOR ME, AND--
--AND YOU'VE NEVER TURNED HIM AWAY, YET HE REMAINS. SO YOU'VE NEVER HAD TO DECIDE WHAT HE IS.
HE LIKES THE UNCERTAINTY...
LIKE YOU.

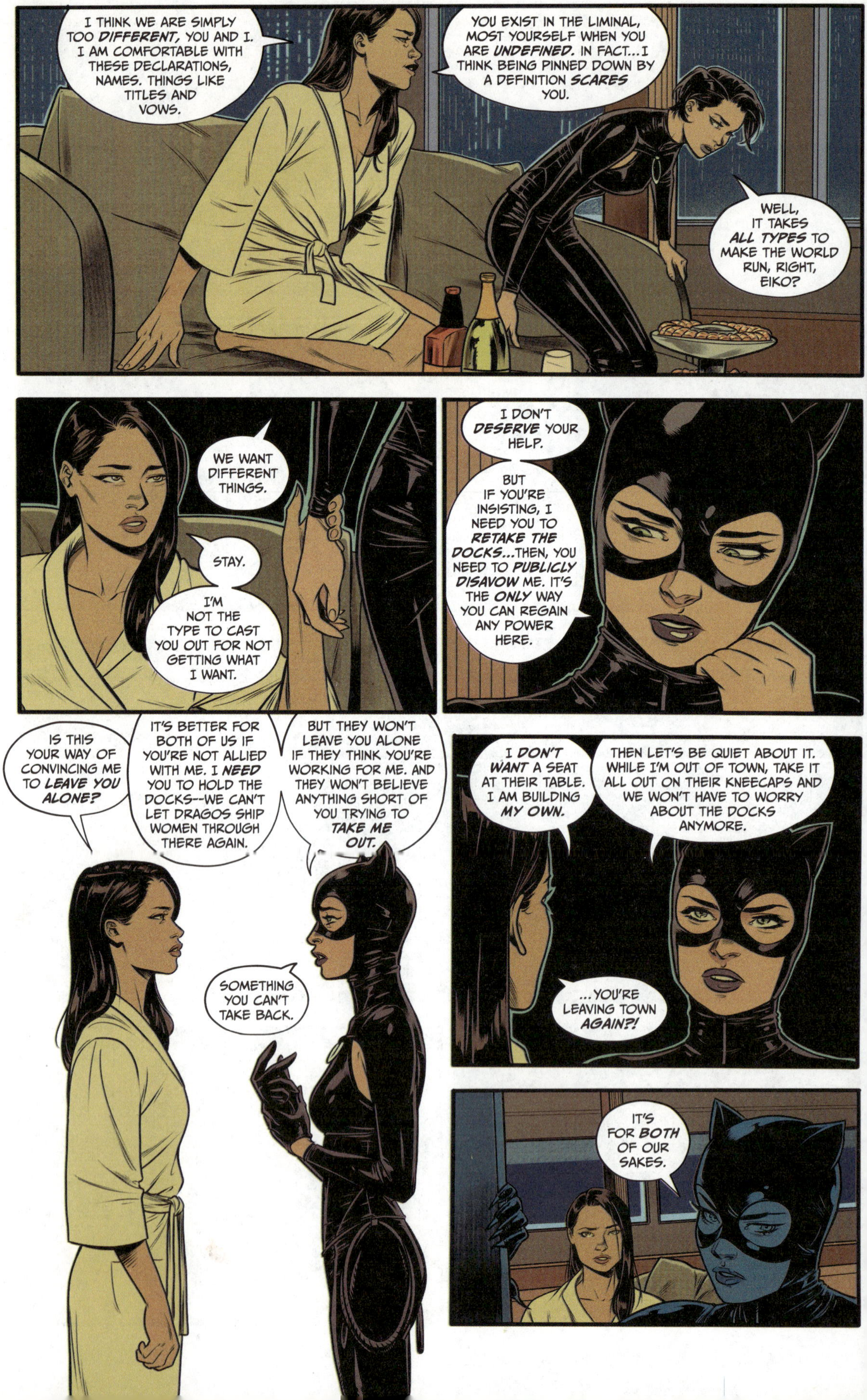
I THINK WE ARE SIMPLY TOO DIFFERENT, YOU AND I. I AM COMFORTABLE WITH THESE DECLARATIONS, NAMES. THINGS LIKE TITLES AND VOWS.
YOU EXIST IN THE LIMINAL, MOST YOURSELF WHEN YOU ARE UNDEFINED. IN FACT...I THINK BEING PINNED DOWN BY A DEFINITION SCARES YOU.
WELL, IT TAKES ALL TYPES TO MAKE THE WORLD RUN, RIGHT, EIKO?
WE WANT DIFFERENT THINGS.
STAY.
I'M NOT THE TYPE TO CAST YOU OUT FOR NOT GETTING WHAT I WANT.
I DON'T DESERVE YOUR HELP.
BUT IF YOU'RE INSISTING, I NEED YOU TO RETAKE THE DOCKS...THEN, YOU NEED TO PUBLICLY DISAVOW ME. IT'S THE ONLY WAY YOU CAN REGAIN ANY POWER HERE.
IS THIS YOUR WAY OF CONVINCING ME TO LEAVE YOU ALONE?
IT'S BETTER FOR BOTH OF US IF YOU'RE NOT ALLIED WITH ME. I NEED YOU TO HOLD THE DOCKS--WE CAN'T LET DRAGOS SHIP WOMEN THROUGH THERE AGAIN.
BUT THEY WON'T LEAVE YOU ALONE IF THEY THINK YOU'RE WORKING FOR ME. AND THEY WON'T BELIEVE ANYTHING SHORT OF YOU TRYING TO TAKE ME OUT.
SOMETHING YOU CAN'T TAKE BACK.
I DON'T WANT A SEAT AT THEIR TABLE. I AM BUILDING MY OWN.
THEN LET'S BE QUIET ABOUT IT. WHILE I'M OUT OF TOWN, TAKE IT ALL OUT ON THEIR KNEECAPS AND WE WON'T HAVE TO WORRY ABOUT THE DOCKS ANYMORE.
...YOU'RE LEAVING TOWN AGAIN?!
IT'S FOR BOTH OF OUR SAKES.

THE NEXT DAY.
Capullo's Meat Market
I APPRECIATE YOU DOIN' SOME GROCERY SHOPPIN' FOR ME.
I DON'T WANT TO BE SEEN IN CAPULLO'S RIGHT NOW. DAD LOVES THAT PLACE.
NOT A PROBLEM. I HAD PLANS TO DO SOME SHOPPING ANYWAY.
MRRRRP?
NOW? WHEN DO YOU SLEEP, WOMAN?
I PROMISE I'LL COME RIGHT HOME AND TAKE A NAP AFTER I'M DONE PICKING UP YOUR MACARONI AND SFOGLIATELLA, DARIO.
CLICK
YOU SOUND--
IF YOU SAY LIKE HIS MOTHER SO HELP ME--
--I WAS GOING TO SAY TIRED AND HUNGRY.
NOW, THIS SHOPPING TOGETHER IS RATHER DOMESTIC, BUT YOU ASKED ME TO MEET YOU HERE "IN A HURRY."
YEAH. I NEED TO GET OUT OF TOWN.

WITH ME?
YOU'RE THE MOST INTERNATIONALLY EQUIPPED PERSON I KNOW. I HAVE A FEELING YOU CAN DO IT FASTER, BETTER, AND MORE COVERTLY THAN EVEN I COULD RIGHT NOW.
I NEED TO GET OUT OF HERE. PREFERABLY ACROSS AN OCEAN.
PASTA PAPA
BUSINESS OR PLEASURE?
...NECESSARY PLEASURE.
MY FAVORITE KIND.
ANY JURISDICTIONS YOU'D LIKE TO AVOID? OUTSTANDING WARRANTS? I DON'T WANT TO BOOK US A TRIP ANYWHERE THAT'S GOING TO GET YOU EXTRADITED.
CRISPY
US?
CAT.
YOU DIDN'T THINK I WAS GOING TO SEND YOU OUT INTO THE WORLD WITHOUT A TRAVELING COMPANION?
DON'T CALL ME CAT. THAT'S... JUST DON'T.
THEN WHAT DO I CALL YOU?
CALL ME... SELINA.
OH! LOVELY NAME.
YOU KNEW.
I DID.

I DON'T NEED A VACATION, I JUST HAD ONE. I WANT TO WORK. YOU CAME HERE TO SEE THE WORLD'S GREATEST THIEF?
SHOW ME THE WORLD'S GREATEST SCORE. AT LEAST, WHATEVER YOU THINK THAT IS.
IS THAT A CHALLENGE TO MY SKILL OR MY ETHICS?
IT'S A... REQUEST? MAYBE A PLEA?
I WANT TO MAKE A DIFFERENCE. FIND ME THAT AND NOTHING LESS.
ANYTHING THE LADY DESIRES.
WHO WILL WATCH THE DUCHESS?
DARIO. HE PRACTICALLY PAYS HIS RENT IN CAT-SITTING HOURS, AND I'LL NEED HIM TO REPORT BACK FROM GOTHAM.
NOW I'VE GOT TO EAT AND SLEEP. EIKO AND I HAVE PLANS TO FINALIZE--I'LL SEND YOU EVERYTHING WE HAVE SO FAR SO YOU KNOW WHERE TO BE, AND WHEN.
OH, YOU'LL NEED MY HELP HERE AS WELL?
VALMONT...
SOMEONE'S GOT TO DRIVE ME TO THE AIRPORT.

CAPULLO'S RISTORANTE.
THANK YOU FOR THE INVITATION.
THANK YOU FOR OBLIGING. BUT I HOPE YOU DIDN'T COME HUNGRY...
KLIK
WE AREN'T STICKING AROUND FOR DINNER.
BAKA.
MY KOBUN IS OUTSIDE AND WILL COME BEHEAD YOU AT A WORD. THAT'S IF YOU SURVIVE MY BLADES. THIS DISRESPECTFUL MONSTER IS WHO YOU WISER MEN ALLY WITH?!
OKAY! FAIR ENOUGH! I JUST WANTED TO GIVE YOU THE CHANCE...
...TO SHOW US WHERE YOU STAND ON THE CAT PROBLEM.
I PREFER TO THINK OF IT AS A COSTUMED CRIMINAL PROBLEM, BLACK MASK.
I FIND HER AS DETESTABLE AS I DO YOU.
PERFECT ANSWER. I MEAN, IF YOU HAD THE CHANCE TO LURE ME INTO A TRAP AND KILL ME...

YOU'D *DO* IT... *RIGHT?*
CALL HER HERE. BRING US THE CAT.
IF I CALL HER IN THE MIDDLE OF THE NIGHT, UNEXPECTEDLY, AND TELL HER TO MEET ME AT A MAFIA HANGOUT?
SHE WOULD *KNOW* WHAT YOU'RE TRYING TO DO.
RIIIINNNG
THIS IS WHY YOU FOOLS WILL NEVER SUCCEED WITHOUT ME.
...EIKO?
CAN YOU MEET ME AT MY YACHT? IT'S ANCHORED IN THE USUAL SPOT.
OF COURSE. ARE YOU OKAY?
...EIKO?
EIKO, DON'T SAY ANYTHING ELSE--I'M ON MY WA--
BEEP
--THERE. SHE'S ON HER WAY. SHALL WE GET TO THE DOCKS IN TIME TO SEE THE SHOW?
I CAN PROMISE... FIREWORKS.
OOOOOHHHH FIIIREWORKS!

WHAT IS YOUR PLAN FOR WHEN SHE ARRIVES?
I CALL A DIFFERENT NUMBER.
I HAVE IT DIALED HERE. I JUST HIT SEND, AND SHE'S DEAD. FIFTY TONS OF EXPLOSIVES ARE PACKED INTO THAT YACHT. IF SHE'S NOT DEAD...SHE'LL WISH SHE WAS.
I DON'T TRUST YOU.
THAT IS WHY I CANNOT LET YOU WORK WITH MY FAMILY, EVER AGAIN, SIONIS.
WE ARE A CLASS OF CRIMINAL WHO RESPECTS EACH OTHER...YOU ARE GUIDED ONLY BY DESIRE, LIKE A STALLION CHASING A MARE.
EIKO--?
SPLISH
...well, it's a convincing betrayal...which is what I asked for...
CATWOMAN.
I'M ON THE PIER, IF YOU'D LIKE TO SEE ME.

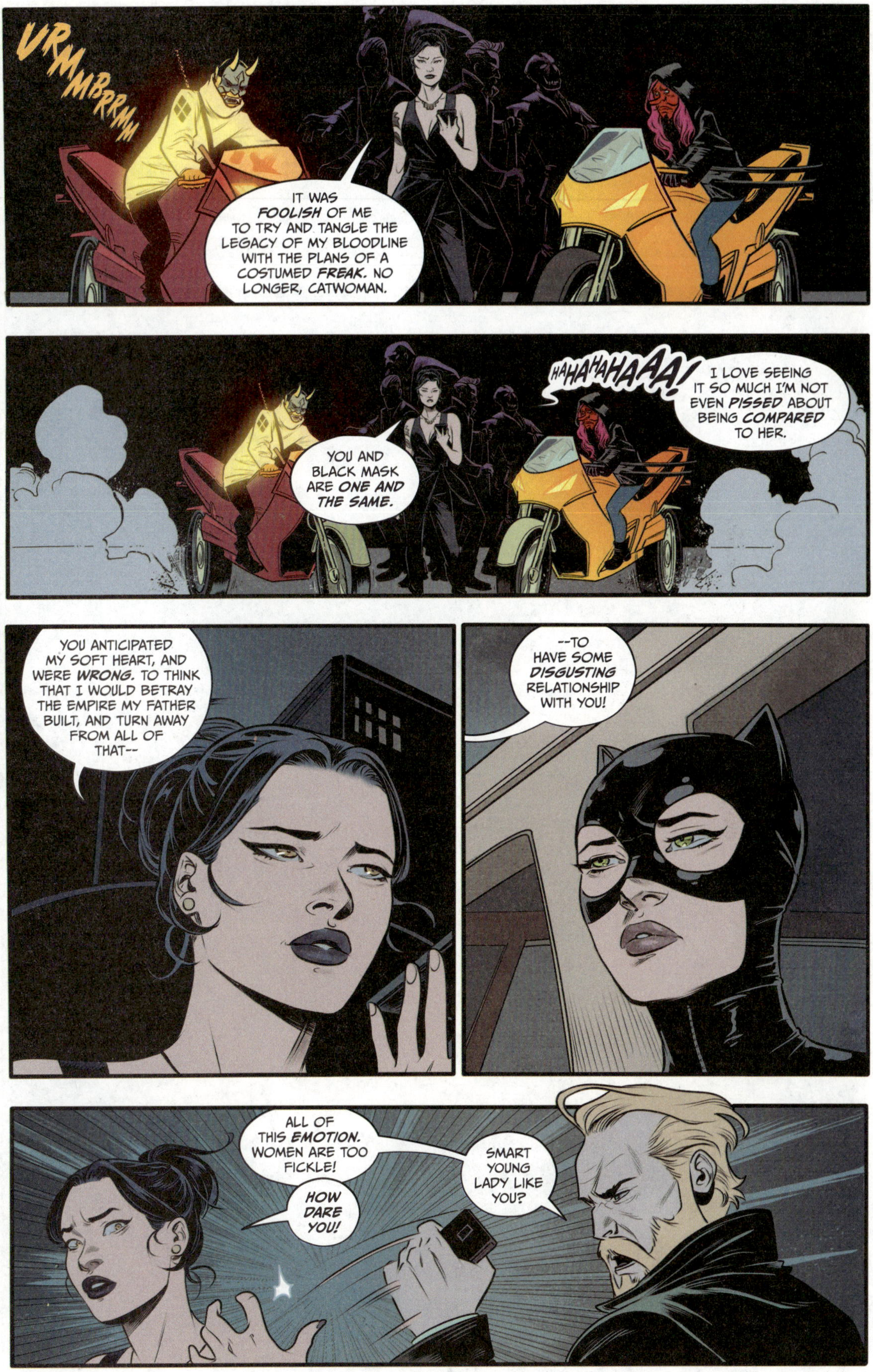

VRMMBRRMM
IT WAS FOOLISH OF ME TO TRY AND TANGLE THE LEGACY OF MY BLOODLINE WITH THE PLANS OF A COSTUMED FREAK. NO LONGER, CATWOMAN.
YOU AND BLACK MASK ARE ONE AND THE SAME.
HAHAHAHAAA! I LOVE SEEING IT SO MUCH I'M NOT EVEN PISSED ABOUT BEING COMPARED TO HER.
YOU ANTICIPATED MY SOFT HEART, AND WERE WRONG. TO THINK THAT I WOULD BETRAY THE EMPIRE MY FATHER BUILT, AND TURN AWAY FROM ALL OF THAT--
--TO HAVE SOME DISGUSTING RELATIONSHIP WITH YOU!
ALL OF THIS EMOTION. WOMEN ARE TOO FICKLE!
SMART YOUNG LADY LIKE YOU?
HOW DARE YOU!

Well, I feel convinced.
--I'LL HELP YOU FIND A BETTER YACHT.
KABOOOOOOOOM
I truly did ask for it...

IS SHE DEAD?
SHE IS DEAD TO ME, AND THE HASIGAWA CLAN.
SHE KNOWS SHE ISN'T WELCOME HERE.
...so why are we crying?
We both know it's not real.
But it had to feel real, to be believable.
Or maybe, there's something in fighting...
...that feels almost as satisfying to me as anything else.
I've never missed anyone I couldn't fight with.
YOU READY?

Sometimes getting passionate is how you know you matter.
Heh, and there's Eiko.
You can't stop a girl from wearing her **favorite outfit.**
No reason to let them **know** I'm out of town.
NEXT: THIEVES WHO STEAL TOGETHER, STAY TOGETHER.

Catwoman #47
1:25 VARIANT COVER BY TULA LOTAY

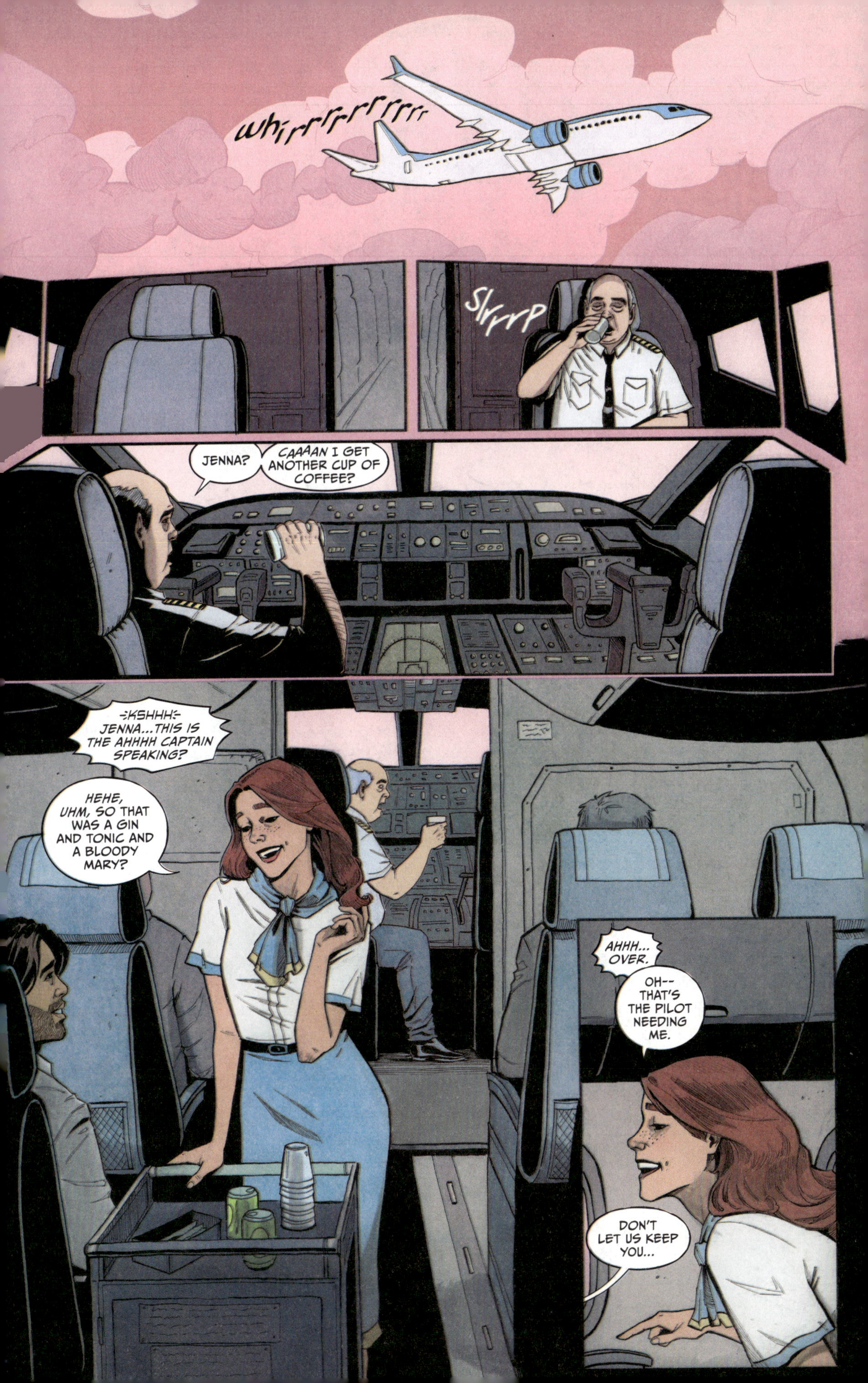
whirrrrrrrrrr
Slrrrp
JENNA?
CAAAAN I GET ANOTHER CUP OF COFFEE?
-KSHHH-
JENNA...THIS IS THE AHHHH CAPTAIN SPEAKING?
HEHE, UHM, SO THAT WAS A GIN AND TONIC AND A BLOODY MARY?
AHHH... OVER.
OH-- THAT'S THE PILOT NEEDING ME.
DON'T LET US KEEP YOU...

CATWOMAN
TINI HOWARD STORY CAITLIN YARSKY ART
JORDIE BELLAIRE COLORS TOM NAPOLITANO & JOSH REED LETT
JEFF DÉKAL COVER SOZOMAIKA VARIANT COVER
TULA LOTAY 1:25 VARIANT COVER JESSICA BERBEY ASSISTANT EDITO
JESSICA CHEN EDITOR BEN ABERNATHY GROUP EDITOR
THOUGH I WOULD IF I *COULD.*
IGNORE THAT ONE. I'M SURE TOO MANY MEN BOTHER YOU IN THIS JOB, ANYWAY.
*OHH-- HEHE...*IT'S NOT A BOTHER AT *ALL...*
I'LL BE RIGHT BACK WITH YOUR DRINKS!
YOU'RE A *SHAMELESS* FLIRT.

ME? I'M GOOD TO EVERY WOMAN--MOST OF THEM DESERVE IT. YOU'RE THE FLIRT.
YOU ARE--
FASCINATING? INTERESTING? DANGEROUS?
SHALL WE UP THE ANTE?
I THINK THE HANDSOME STEWARD WHO BROUGHT OUR PRETZELS MIGHT SETTLE THIS ARGUMENT FOR US.
FUN.
BUT I'LL WARN YOU--I DON'T VACATION WELL. ESPECIALLY WHEN I DON'T YET KNOW WHERE WE'RE GOING.
JUST BECAUSE YOU'RE GORGEOUS AND WE'RE IN FIRST CLASS DOESN'T MEAN I WON'T DECIDE I'M BEING KIDNAPPED.
SO I ENCOURAGE YOU TO BE FORTHCOMING, VALMONT.
HH
FIRST? SWITZERLAND. A LOVELY LITTLE SKI CHALET...
...WHERE FINBAR SULLIVAN'S BROTHER DECLAN SPENDS HIS VACATIONS.
THEN, VIENNA. THE IBANESCU FAMILY FINDS ROMANIAN BANKING TOO UNSTABLE FOR THEIR LARGE AMOUNTS OF LIQUIDITY, BUT AUSTRIA SERVES JUST FINE.
LOVELY CITY, HOWEVER, I DON'T NEED TO BE MESSING WITH FINBAR SULLIVAN.
THANKS TO ONYX'S HELP, THEIR LITTLE IRISH BOXING RING IS ONE OF THE ONLY CRIME FAMILIES THAT DOESN'T CAUSE ME TROUBLE IN GOTHAM. FINBAR'S IN MY POCKET.
AND SECONDLY...

...YOU COULDN'T PICK *ANYWHERE* WARM?
IF YOU *LIKE* FINBAR, YOU'LL *DEFINITELY* WANT TO BE HERE TO MEET DECLAN. BECAUSE DECLAN...DOESN'T LIKE WHAT HE'S HEARING.
THAT FINBAR *KNEELS* TO YOU.
FROM WHAT I UNDERSTAND ABOUT *DECLAN*...HE ISN'T IN ANY SHAPE TO TAKE OVER THE FAMILY.
NO. BUT *ABIGAIL* IS.
Received
From
Crime
Date of Sentence
Location
Date of Birth
Weight
Age
Occupation
CRIMINAL HISTORY
Declan was a boxer, like his brother.
But he wasn't a very **good** one, meaning he took too many hits to the head. Enter his **wife**--
Abigail remains **sharp as a tack** and is rumored to handle most of Declan's men, missions, and **business** herself.
Declan is Abigail's puppet. No reason she wouldn't want to make **Finbar** one, too.
VALMONT, IF YOU BROUGHT ME ALL THE WAY HERE JUST TO TELL ME THINGS I *ALREADY* KNOW...
AH, BUT YOU NEEDED *ME*--

--TO KNOW THEY'D BE HERE.
I GUESS THAT IS USEFUL.
AND I DO LOVE HOT CHOCOLATE.
PURRRR THAT'S DELICIOUS.
WOULD IT MAKE YOU FEEL BETTER IF I TOLD YOU I DON'T KNOW WHO THE MAN THEY'RE TALKING TO IS? YOU CAN TELL ME ABOUT HIM.
HMMM...
THAT I DON'T KNOW.
LET ME SEE WHAT I CAN DO ABOUT THAT.
brrr
DARIO

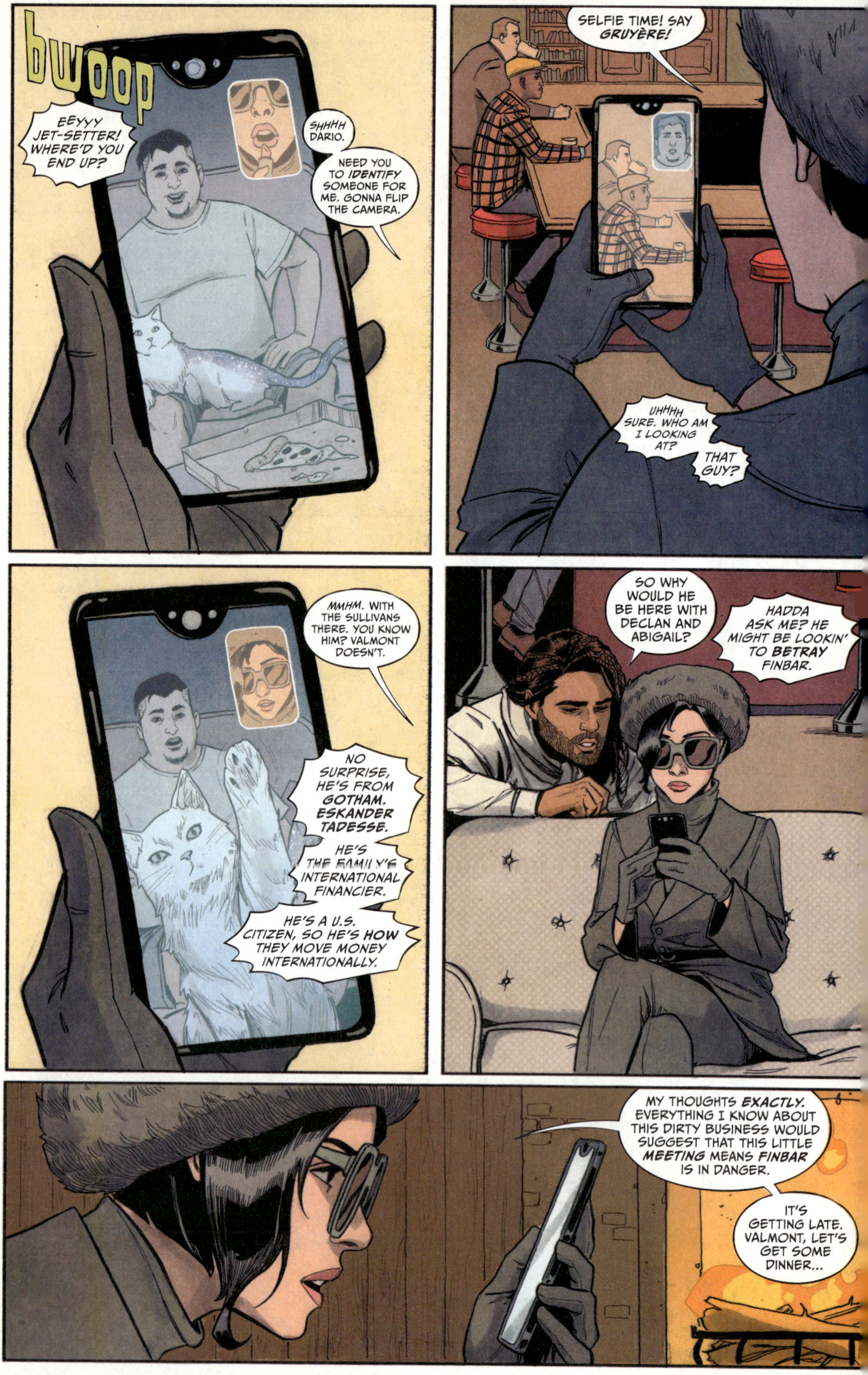
bwoop
EEyyy JET-SETTER! WHERE'D YOU END UP?
SHHHH DARIO.
NEED YOU TO IDENTIFY SOMEONE FOR ME. GONNA FLIP THE CAMERA.
SELFIE TIME! SAY GRUYÈRE!
UHHHH SURE. WHO AM I LOOKING AT?
THAT GUY?
MMHM. WITH THE SULLIVANS THERE. YOU KNOW HIM? VALMONT DOESN'T.
NO SURPRISE, HE'S FROM GOTHAM. ESKANDER TADESSE.
HE'S THE FAMILY'S INTERNATIONAL FINANCIER.
HE'S A U.S. CITIZEN, SO HE'S HOW THEY MOVE MONEY INTERNATIONALLY.
SO WHY WOULD HE BE HERE WITH DECLAN AND ABIGAIL?
HADDA ASK ME? HE MIGHT BE LOOKIN' TO BETRAY FINBAR.
MY THOUGHTS EXACTLY. EVERYTHING I KNOW ABOUT THIS DIRTY BUSINESS WOULD SUGGEST THAT THIS LITTLE MEETING MEANS FINBAR IS IN DANGER.
IT'S GETTING LATE. VALMONT, LET'S GET SOME DINNER...

"...AND I'LL GO HAVE A TALK WITH HIM TONIGHT."
NOW WHAT SORT OF AMENITIES COME IN THE INTERNATIONAL CRIME FINANCE MANAGER SUITE, I WONDER...
SHHHHK
He seems on edge.
I feel a little bad about that.
AAAH--

DON'T. MOVE.
Aahhh-- NOO! DON'T!
I WILL.
IF YOU DON'T TELL ME ABOUT WHAT YOU'RE DOING FOR ABIGAIL AND DECLAN SULLIVAN WITHOUT FINBAR'S KNOWLEDGE.
CATWOMAN, PLEASE!
I'M HONESTLY THRILLED TO SEE YOU! MAY I SAY--I AM A FAN OF YOUR INFLUENCE ON MY CLIENT.
...THAT'S A PLEASANT SURPRISE.
BUT I SUSPECT ABIGAIL AND DECLAN...ARE NOT. I THINK THEY INVITED ME HERE... TO KILL ME!

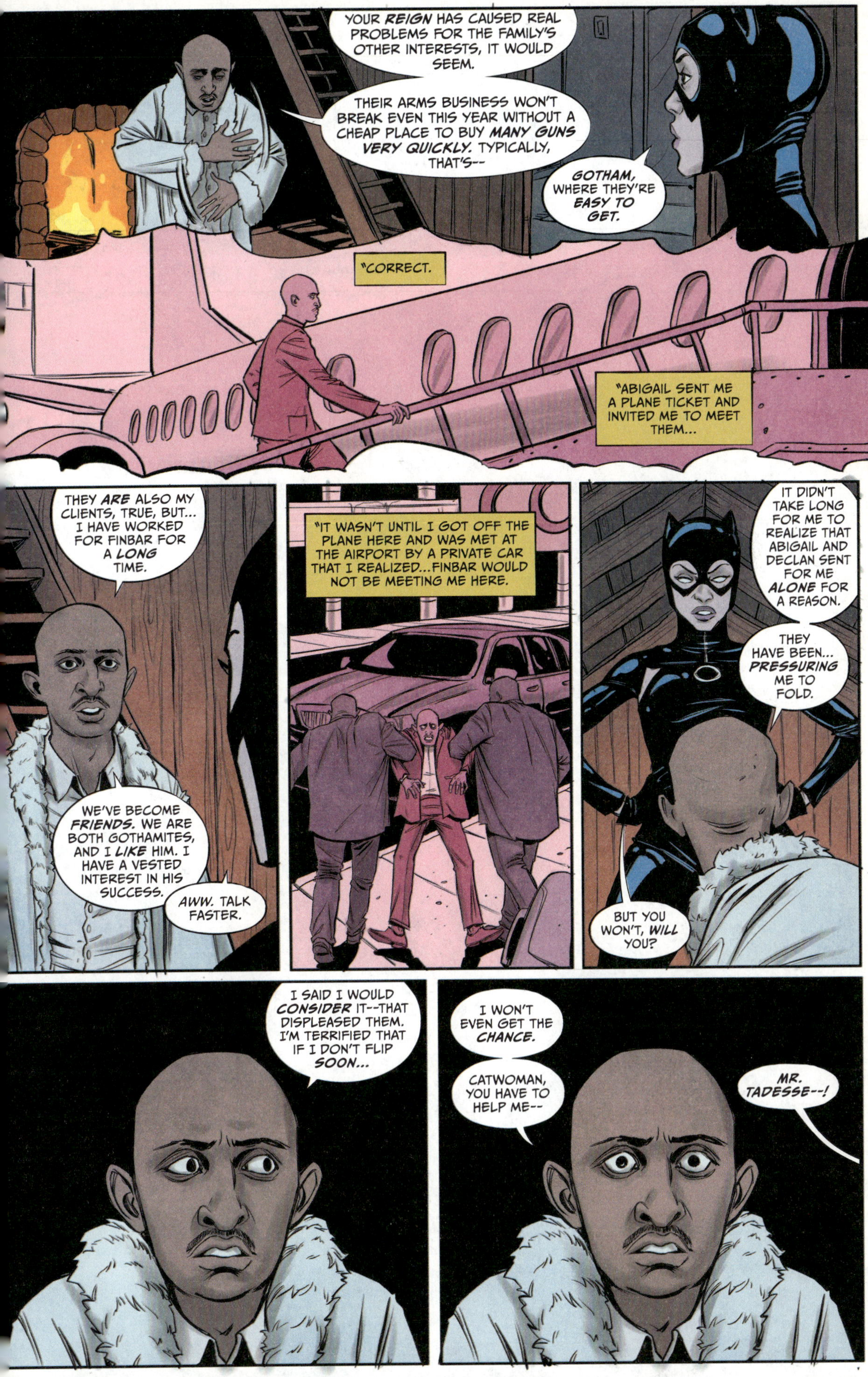
YOUR **REIGN** HAS CAUSED REAL PROBLEMS FOR THE FAMILY'S OTHER INTERESTS, IT WOULD SEEM.
THEIR ARMS BUSINESS WON'T BREAK EVEN THIS YEAR WITHOUT A CHEAP PLACE TO BUY **MANY GUNS VERY QUICKLY.** TYPICALLY, THAT'S--
GOTHAM, WHERE THEY'RE **EASY TO GET.**
"CORRECT.
"ABIGAIL SENT ME A PLANE TICKET AND INVITED ME TO MEET THEM...
THEY **ARE** ALSO MY CLIENTS, TRUE, BUT... I HAVE WORKED FOR FINBAR FOR A **LONG** TIME.
WE'VE BECOME **FRIENDS.** WE ARE BOTH GOTHAMITES, AND I **LIKE** HIM. I HAVE A VESTED INTEREST IN HIS SUCCESS.
AWW. TALK FASTER.
"IT WASN'T UNTIL I GOT OFF THE PLANE HERE AND WAS MET AT THE AIRPORT BY A PRIVATE CAR THAT I REALIZED...FINBAR WOULD NOT BE MEETING ME HERE.
IT DIDN'T TAKE LONG FOR ME TO REALIZE THAT ABIGAIL AND DECLAN SENT FOR ME **ALONE** FOR A REASON.
THEY HAVE BEEN... **PRESSURING** ME TO FOLD.
BUT YOU WON'T, **WILL** YOU?
I SAID I WOULD **CONSIDER** IT--THAT DISPLEASED THEM. I'M TERRIFIED THAT IF I DON'T FLIP **SOON...**
I WON'T EVEN GET THE **CHANCE.**
CATWOMAN, YOU HAVE TO HELP ME--
MR. TADESSE--!

WHY DON'T YOU COME OUTSIDE...SO WE CAN SPARE THOSE LOVELY CHALET WINDOWS?
BDDDTT DTTT DTT BDDT
GET DOWN!
AAAHHH!
VALMONT!
BRRRMRMM
THEY'RE GOING TO KILL ME!
I COULD'VE JUST WORKED ON WALL STREET LIKE MY MOTHER WANTED...
THEY'RE ATTEMPTING IT. I'VE BEEN FOLLOWING THEM.
HURRY, WE CAN OUTRUN THE SKIERS ON THIS, BUT WE HAVE GO-- NOW!

GOTHAM CITY, THE TRIXIE, SELINA'S APARTMENT.
MROW?
WHAT?!
MRROWROW.
thump
OKAY, DON'T BE SO SENSITIVE! JEEZ.
WHAT. OH...YOU WANT ME TO WORK ON THAT.
YEAH. I BEEN THINKING ABOUT FINISHING THAT UP TOO.
GONNA WAIT TILL SELINA GETS BACK, THOUGH. I DON'T WANT ANYONE THINKING I'M UNDERMININ' HER, YANNO?
MRRRR.
I WAS GONNA HONOR HER. LIKE GO BOY...STRAYBOY OR TOMCAT OR... SOMETHIN' BETTER.
MRR.
OH, YOU THINK SHE'LL BE MAD? WELL, I CAN'T BE HERE BY MYSELF FOR SO LONG AND NOT DO NOTHIN' ABOUT IT!

OH. YOU JUST WANTED CAT FOOD.
THAT'S ON ME THEN. CALL IT CAT'LIC GUILT.
LEMME RUN DOWN TO THE BODEGA AND GET YOU A CAN A'CAT FOOD.
M-RROW!
ding
HOLD THAT, PLEASE--
HEY, THANKS, GOT A HUNGRY CAT BACK THERE.
OH, THAT CAT'S GONNA STAY HUNGRY.
NOAH?!
ABOUT THAT--I BEEN THINKIN'. YOU KNOW WAY TOO MUCH ABOUT US TO BE THAT COMFORTABLE WITH CATWOMAN. CALL IT A LOOSE END TO TIE UP, BABY--I MEAN, @#$%--DARIO.
OLD HABITS DIE HARD. BUT YOU? YOU'RE GONNA DIE REAL EASY.
CLIK

WILL I BE ABLE TO GET ANYTHING ELSE FROM MY ROOM?
NO! WIPE YOUR ELECTRONICS FROM A DISTANCE AND BUY NEW SUITS!
WE'LL GET YOU TO SAFETY, BUT WE HAVE TO LOSE THOSE SNIPERS, FIRST!
THE SKIERS, WE'LL LOSE THEM ANY MINUTE NOW--THEY CAN'T KEEP UP WITH US AND SHOOT, EVEN DOWNHILL.
BANG BANG BANG
LOOK OUT!
ALL BECAUSE I WOULDN'T BETRAY *FINBAR!* WELL I WON'T BE HELPING *THEM, NOW THAT THEY ARE GOING TO KILL ME!*
THAT'S NOT GOING TO HAPPEN--WE'RE HEADED FOR SAFETY, I PROMISE YOU, MR. TADESSE!
BRRRMRMM
I HEAR ANOTHER SNOWMOBILE!

CH-CHK
BRRRRMRMM
THAT'S IT. I'M TIRED OF BEING THREE IN A POD.
HE'S GAINING!
LET HIM GAIN.
CATWOMAN?!
SO IT'S TRUE, SULLIVAN IS YOUR @#$%^ NOW!
KRAK
OOF!
CATWOMAN. ARE YOU STILL JOINING US?

CATWOMAN?!
ONE MOMENT PLEASE!
I'VE MY PHONE, I CAN CALL--
DON'T. EVERYTHING OF YOURS IS BEING TRACKED, I'M SURE OF IT.
I HAVE COVERT CONNECTIONS IN THIS PART OF THE WORLD.
I'VE GOT HELICOPTERS READY TO MAKE A SNOW LANDING ANY MINUTE NOW!
FWP FWP FWP
THERE SHE IS!
LET'S GET OUT OF HERE-- LIKE OUT OF THE COUNTRY HERE.
WE'LL HAVE TO REFUEL THE HELICOPTER BETWEEN HERE AND VIENNA.
FWP FWP FWP
PERFECT. ESKANDER--YOUR CHOPPER WILL BE HERE RIGHT AFTER OURS, BUT WE NEED TO MOVE SO THEY CAN MAKE THE LANDING.
CHECK IN AS SOON AS YOU'RE IN THE AIR SO WE KNOW YOU'RE SAFE.
HAPPY TO, CATWOMAN. AND VALMONT-- THANK YOU BOTH. I AM SORRY TO BRING SO MUCH STRESS AND CHAOS TO YOUR VACATION.
NO APOLOGY NEEDED.
I DON'T THINK THIS WAS GOING TO BE A RESTFUL ONE, ANYWAY.

ding
WALK REAL NORMAL.
HOW CAN I ACT NORMAL AT A TIME LIKE THIS?
YOU NEVER WALKED THIS CLOSE TO ME IN PUBLIC BEFORE.
SHUDDUP.
IN.
YOU'RE KIDDIN' ME.
COURSE NOT. I GOT A DRIVER AND EVERYTHING. IN THE TRUNK.
YOU AREN'T GONNA KILL ME, NOAH. C'MON.
YOU WOULDA DONE IT ALREADY.
AND IT WON'T CHANGE WHO YOU ARE, OR WHAT WE DID TOGETHER. I... STILL LOVE YOU, NOAH--
THUNK

VIENNA, AUSTRIA.
THE CRAP I TOOK FROM POP FOR WANTING TWO PHONES AND NOW IT'S GONNA SAVE MY #@$%-$@ LIFE.
rrrng
...SELINA, PLEASE...
...PICK UP YOUR PHONE!
YOU'RE SURE THEY'RE HERE, VALMONT?
CRASH
I PROMISED YOU A SCORE, ONE THAT WOULD MAKE A DIFFERENCE, NO?
YOU SAID THE RECORDS ROBIN HAD, OF WOMEN BEING SOLD AS PAINTINGS, WERE NOT ENOUGH TO STOP MR. IBANESCU'S TRAFFICKING?
THEY WERE DEEMED CIRCUMSTANTIAL. AND THOSE GIRLS AREN'T GOING TO TESTIFY-- AND THEY SHOULDN'T HAVE TO.

THEY HAVE TO KEEP REAL RECORDS WRITTEN DOWN SOMEWHERE--THESE MEN DON'T TRUST EACH OTHER THAT MUCH.
BUT THEY ARE ALL HANDWRITTEN. OLD-WORLD. THE ONLY WAY THEY TRUST.
THESE ARE...DISGUSTING. BUT THEY'RE EXACTLY WHAT WE NEED.
HOW DID YOU KNOW THESE WERE HERE?
CONTACT OF MINE.
YOU HAVE A CONTACT WHO KNEW THESE WERE HERE, AND DIDN'T DO ANYTHING ABOUT IT?
HOW LONG DID YOU KNOW ABOUT IT?
ALLOW ME TO EXPLAIN--
THESE ARE WOMEN'S LIVES!
HOW LONG?!

THUMP
THUMP
IF IT WERE THE POLICE THEY WOULD HAVE THE KEYS...
THUMP
THUMP
SO THE VIENNA IBANESCUS MUST HAVE HEARD WE WERE HITTING THEIR FAVORITE BANK.
THUMP
WHAT ARE YOU DOING?
LETTING THEM IN--
WHAT THE HELL?!

YOU TRY AND LOCK US OUT OF OUR OWN VAULT?
THERE ISN'T ENOUGH MONEY IN HERE TO MAKE IT WORTH HOW BADLY WE'RE GOING TO HURT YOU.
I TAKE THE ONE ON THE RIGHT...
...YOU TAKE THE LEFT?
--AND SPARE THE FOOL IN THE MIDDLE...
...TO RUN BACK AND TELL THEM.
HUH?!
SWISH
WHOOSH
AAAAH!
THUK

HUP--
I COULD SAY THE SAME--
YOU'RE LUCKY I DON'T BEAT YOU TO DEATH WITH A BAG OF JEWELS FOR YOUR GREED!
THWAT
---BUT IT WOULDN'T LEAVE A SCAR.
SLASH
AAHHHGHH!
EEOOOEEOOOEEOOOOE
TELL ME THOSE AREN'T SIRENS.
EEOOOEEOOOEEOO
WELL LET'S HURRY BEFORE WE END UP HAVING TO CALL AN EMBASSY TO RESCUE US?
I CALL THE CONTACT THAT IS OF THE MOST USE TO ME AT THE MOMENT.

YOUR CONTACT WAS IN *INTERPOL?*
THEY DIDN'T HAVE THE EVIDENCE TO MOVE IN... UNLESS, OF COURSE... SOMEONE **ROBBED** THAT BANK...
NOT BAD, VALMONT.
OH NO, I'M ONLY JUST NOW GETTING SERVICE.
*CATOMAN! **NOAH'S** GOT ME. I'M IN THE TRUNK OF HIS CAR. HE'S GONNA **KILL** ME. I DON'T CARE THAT THIS ISN'T **SECURE**.*
THERE'S NO WAY--THE FLIGHT WOULD BE **TEN HOURS** AND THAT'S IF WE GOT ONE **NOW**. THEY'LL ***KILL*** HIM WHILE WE'RE IN THE AIR.
CATWOMAN, PLEASE!
*I DON'T KNOW WHERE IN EUROPE YOU ARE, BUT I HAVE AN **AUNT MIA** IN **TUSCANY...** I ALWAYS TRUSTED **HER**.*
YOU HAVE TO CANCEL WHATEVER YOU HAD PLANNED, VALMONT.
WE'RE GOING TO *ITALY* TO SAVE DARIO'S LIFE.
NEXT:
CAT-CH
ME IF YOU CA

CATWOMAN #48
1:25 VARIANT COVER BY TULA LOTAY

TUSCANY
Sometimes when I say it, I'm being cute.
CATWOMAN
FURIOUS HEARTS PART 1 OF 3
TINI HOWARD STORY NICO LEON ART
VERONICA GANDINI COLORS JOSH REED LETTERS
JEFF DÉKAL COVER SOZOMAIKA VARIANT COVER
TULA LOTAY 1:25 RATIO VARIANT COVER
JESSICA BERBEY ASSISTANT EDITOR
JESSICA CHEN EDITOR
BEN ABERNATHY GROUP EDITOR
--and sometimes, admittedly, I'm flirting.
But tonight... I mean it.
NO TALKING UNTIL I SAY SO, VALMONT.
WE'RE HERE TO SAVE DARIO, AND THESE PEOPLE WON'T HESITATE TO MAKE IT A MATTER OF LIFE AND DEATH.
I WOULD KNOW.

...they're just like my family.
MISS SELINA CALABRESE?
THANK YOU.
SIGNORE?
PLEASE, CALL ME VAL.
YOU BETTER NOT GIVE THE VALETS YOUR ONLY KEY. WE MIGHT NEED TO DRIVE OUT OF HERE ON A MOMENT'S NOTICE.
ANY MORE ORDERS? I CONFESS I LIKE DOING WHAT YOU SAY.
SELINA?
...YOU MUST BE HER, THE FAMILY RESEMBLANCE IS STRONG.
I'M MIA TOMASSO.
PARK THE CAR, GENTLEMEN. I'LL TAKE SELINA AND VAL FOR A TOUR. GO AHEAD AND HAVE THE STAFF PREPARE US SOMETHING FAR MERENDA WHEN WE RETURN.
MIA TOMASSO...
DARIO'S AUNT MIA?
...SHALL WE GO INSIDE?

NOT YET. INSIDE...WE WON'T BE ABLE TO SPEAK AS FREELY.
...THEN YOU KNOW?
...KNOW WHAT?
ABOUT DARIO?
HE'S IN DANGER. WE DON'T HAVE TIME FAR MERENDA.
OH, DON'T I KNOW IT.
YOU MIGHT KNOW ALREADY-- I'M NOT REALLY DARIO'S AUNT. BUT I WAS BEST FRIENDS WITH HIS MAMA FROM WAY BACK--WE WERE SENT TO SCHOOL TOGETHER. WHEN I MARRIED ONE OF THE DON'S COUSINS, WE BECAME FAMILY.
BUT HIS MAMA AND I WERE...CLOSE, ONCE UPON A TIME.
--IMMEDIATE DANGER, MIA.
HIS FATHER AND NOAH, THEY'VE BETRAYED HIM FOR GOOD. THEY'VE MADE A MOVE AND HE'S IN CAPTIVITY.
I HEAR YOU, SELINA.
BUT HERE, WE WORK BY TRADITION.
CAN YOU HELP US OR NOT?
PLEASE--
--COME INSIDE, AND I'LL SEE WHAT WE CAN DO.

VILLA TOMASSO.
MAY I INTRODUCE, OF COURSE, MISS SELINA CALABRESE, AND HER TRAVELING COMPANION, VAL.
THIS IS DON LORENZO TOMASSO, AND HIS WIFE VITTORIA.
SELINA.
YOU COME FAMIGLIA CALABRESE?
NO.
I'M NOT HERE ABOUT MY FAMILY.
I'M HERE ABOUT YOURS.
THE TOMASSOS OF GOTHAM HAVE TAKEN ONE OF MY ALLIES HOSTAGE. HIS NAME IS DARIO TOMASSO, AND I'D LIKE HIM FREED.
TOMASSO.
ALLOW ME, DARLING.
SOUNDS LIKE FAMILY BUSINESS. MEANING NO ONE OUTSIDE OF US SHOULD HAVE A DAMN THING TO SAY ABOUT IT.

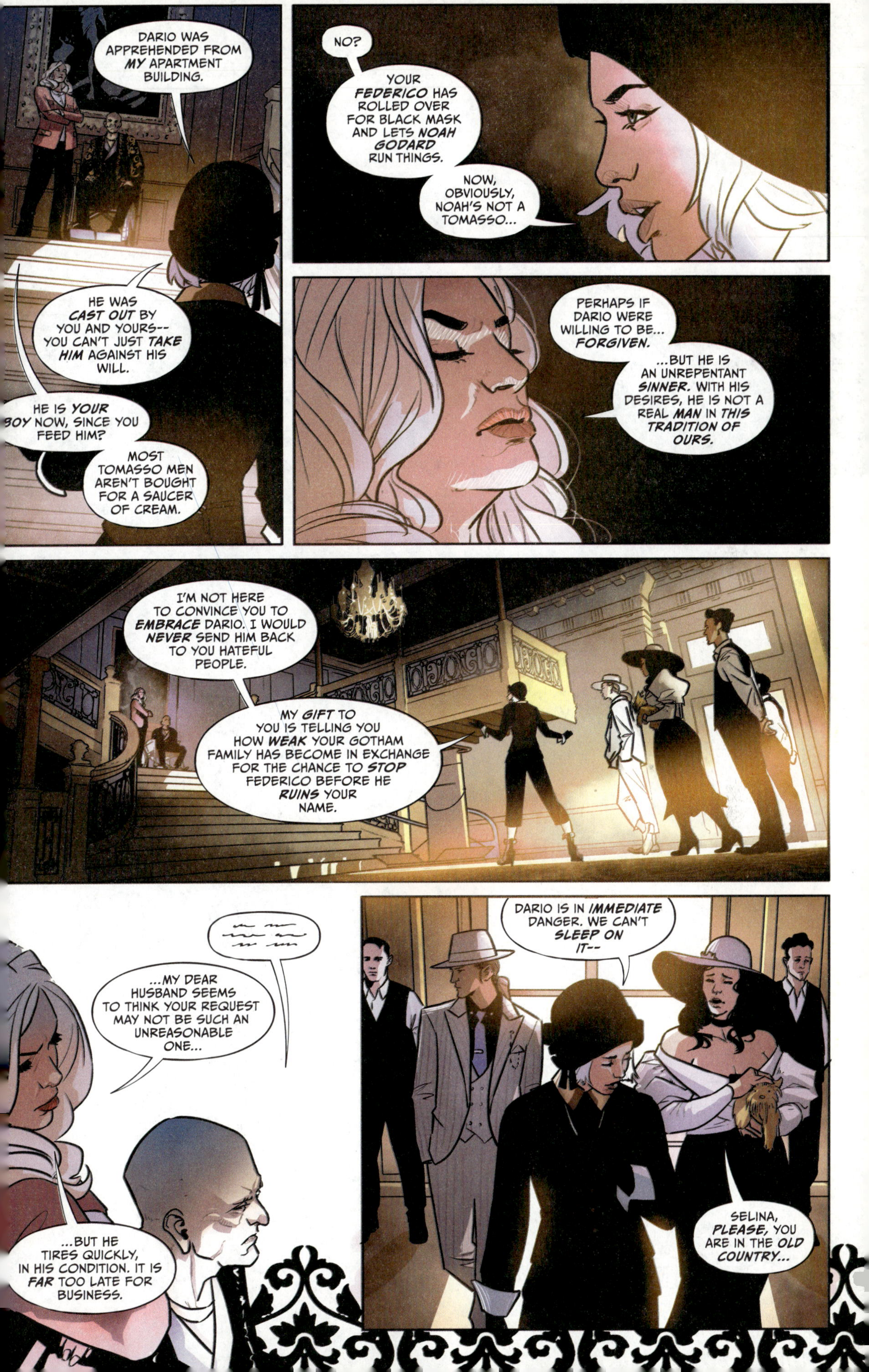
DARIO WAS APPREHENDED FROM MY APARTMENT BUILDING.
NO?
YOUR FEDERICO HAS ROLLED OVER FOR BLACK MASK AND LETS NOAH GODARD RUN THINGS.
NOW, OBVIOUSLY, NOAH'S NOT A TOMASSO...
HE WAS CAST OUT BY YOU AND YOURS-- YOU CAN'T JUST TAKE HIM AGAINST HIS WILL.
HE IS YOUR BOY NOW, SINCE YOU FEED HIM?
MOST TOMASSO MEN AREN'T BOUGHT FOR A SAUCER OF CREAM.
PERHAPS IF DARIO WERE WILLING TO BE... FORGIVEN.
...BUT HE IS AN UNREPENTANT SINNER. WITH HIS DESIRES, HE IS NOT A REAL MAN IN THIS TRADITION OF OURS.
I'M NOT HERE TO CONVINCE YOU TO EMBRACE DARIO. I WOULD NEVER SEND HIM BACK TO YOU HATEFUL PEOPLE.
MY GIFT TO YOU IS TELLING YOU HOW WEAK YOUR GOTHAM FAMILY HAS BECOME IN EXCHANGE FOR THE CHANCE TO STOP FEDERICO BEFORE HE RUINS YOUR NAME.
...MY DEAR HUSBAND SEEMS TO THINK YOUR REQUEST MAY NOT BE SUCH AN UNREASONABLE ONE...
...BUT HE TIRES QUICKLY, IN HIS CONDITION. IT IS FAR TOO LATE FOR BUSINESS.
DARIO IS IN IMMEDIATE DANGER. WE CAN'T SLEEP ON IT--
SELINA, PLEASE, YOU ARE IN THE OLD COUNTRY...

GOTHAM CITY. NOW.
"...SOME THINGS MUST BE DONE THE SLOW WAY."
SO GOOD TO SEE YOU OUT AND ABOUT, MAN. HONESTLY, I APPRECIATE YOU COMING OUT FROM YOUR BOILER ROOM TO MEET WITH ME.
...WHERE IS HE?
IN THE TRUNK. DON'T WORRY--
I GAVE HIM SOME "PAIN PILLS" EARLIER-- HE SHOULD BE OUT COLD.
MMNH. SHOULD HAVE JUST SHOT 'IM.
OH, @#$%.
I KNOW THAT VOICE.
I THOUGHT I'D SAVE THAT PLEASURE FOR YOU. IF I HAND HIM OVER TO YOU.
...IF?
DON TOMASSO MAY HAVE MADE THE DEAL, BUT HE ASKED ME TO DELIVER THE GOODS. WHICH MEANS YOU HAVE TO TIP ME FOR THE DELIVERY.
YOU WANT TO PLAY AT BEING A REAL MADE MAN, BUT YOU DON'T KNOW THE FIRST THING ABOUT HOW WE OPERATE. I WOULD KNOW--I FOUGHT MY WAY INTO THIS FAMIGLIA FROM THE OUTSIDE, AND I WON'T LET SOME INSANE THUG IN A MASK TELL ME WHAT TO DO.
YOU WANT DARIO TOMASSO? THAT'S A BIG PIECE ON THE BOARD.
TELL ME WHAT HE'S WORTH TO YOU.
hey hrruy

its balck fckugni mask
HHHH... HHHHH... NOAH GODARD...
...YOU ALMOST REMIND ME OF MY OLD SELF...'CEPT I NEVER WAS A @#$%.
THOUGH YOU DO GOT A PAIR! THERE ISN'T A SOLID PAIR OF @$%@^# IN THAT ENTIRE FAMILY.
NOW THAT YOU GOT 'EM, LEMME SHOW YOU WHAT YOU DO WITH 'EM--
WHO YOU CALLING A @#$%?
BLAM BLAM
AH!
FIRST THINGS FIRST--
BRATTATATAT
DON'T THINK FOR A SECOND THAT I DON'T KNOW YOU HAVE SOME LINGERING SENSE OF MERCY FOR YOUR LITTLE BOYFRIEND HERE AND I THINK THAT IS JUST PATHETIC.
CAREFUL, ROMAN. HE'S THE SON OF THE DON--HE'S NOT LIKE YOUR STRING OF DISPOSABLE MISTRESSES.
OOOF!
EVERYONE'S DISPOSABLE, KID. EVEN DARIO.
BUT HE'S THE PERFECT THING TO TAKE TO GET BACK AT THE CAT!

TUSCANY.
TIME TO GET UP.
WE'VE GOT WORK TO DO.
CAN I CONVINCE YOU TO STAY?
I CAN'T SLEEP RIGHT NOW.
...I DIDN'T INTEND FOR US TO SLEEP.
SHH. NOT NOW.
DARIO'S STILL IN DANGER. BLACK MASK BETRAYED NOAH AND TOOK HIM HOSTAGE.
I HAVE ONE LAST THING I HAVE TO DO HERE, BUT THEN OUR VACATION'S OVER. WE'RE GOING BACK TO GOTHAM.
HEH. THEY SAY CATS MAKE POOR MOTHERS, YET YOU CAN'T HELP BUT CARE, SELINA.
I HAVE TO.
GIVE YOURSELF MORE CREDIT, MA CHATTE--
--YOU WANT TO.

DO YOU TRUST MIA?
NOT A *CHANCE.* WE MAY HAVE TO ACCEPT THAT SHE WAS ONLY USEFUL FOR GETTING US IN THE DOOR.
PEOPLE THAT LIVE IN FANCY HOUSES LIKE THIS DON'T WANT TO THROW STONES AROUND WHEN THE TIME COMES.
SHE *CARES* ABOUT DARIO, BUT SHE'S TOO INTENT ON *KEEPING THE PEACE* TO DO ANYTHING ABOUT IT?
REAL LOVE MEANS DESTROYING THE PEACE SOMETIMES.
I'M MEANT FOR *PASSION,* NOT *PEACE.*
IT CAN BE A LITTLE NAIVE TO TRY AND HAVE BOTH.
THAT'S WHY WE GET ALONG.
WE BOTH WANT *IMPOSSIBLE* THINGS.

YOU'RE TOO LATE.
SNRRF
BLACK MASK HAS TAKEN DARIO. GODARD LOST HIM.
THERE'S NOTHING TO BE DONE FROM HERE BUT FOR YOU TO HEAD BACK TO GOTHAM AND--
TT TT HERE BOY.
NICE TRY, BUT I KNOW YOUR TYPE.
YOU DON'T WANT TO LET THEM SAY DISGUSTING THINGS ABOUT DARIO...BUT NOT SO MUCH THAT YOU'LL PUT YOURSELF OUT OF FAVOR WHAT A BEAUTIFUL VILLA YOU HAVE HERE.
DOLCI
PUT HIM DOWN.
LET US IN.
OR DOLCI BECOMES MY CAT TOY.
YOU'RE A MONSTER.
BEEP BEEP
OH PLEASE, YOU WEREN'T PERSUADED BY YOUR OWN NEPHEW IN DANGER.
YOU'RE IN. BUT YOU WON'T GET OUT ALIVE.

GOOD EVENING, TOMASSOS. BUSINESS NEVER SLEEPS.
CATWOMAN?!
GUAARRDS =HKK-KOFF=
MY COHORT MS. CALABRESE SAID YOU TWO WERE BEING DIFFICULT AND CALLED IN HER FAVOR. I HEAR DARIO IS NOW IN THE HANDS OF BLACK MASK. GOING TO BE PRETTY EMBARRASSING FOR THE DON IF HIS ONLY SO ENDS UP TORTURED BY A COSTUMED CRIMINAL, ISN'T IT?

MY HUSBAND CAN BARELY SPEAK. WITH WHAT AUTHORITY AM I TO CALL THE DON IN GOTHAM CITY AND GIVE HIM ORDERS?!
RECOGNIZE THIS?
...THE... BLACK GLOVE?
THE SAME.
BUT HERE IT IS WITH ME, WHICH IS A PROBLEM. NOW, THE LOVELY MIA TOLD ME THAT OUT HERE, IN THE OLD COUNTRY, WE FOLLOW THE OLD TRADITIONS, NO MATTER HOW STUPID.
ISN'T IT TRUE THAT WHOEVER HOLDS THE BLACK GLOVE LEADS THE TOMASSO FAMILY?
DON'T KILL ME--
I'M OFFERING YOU SOMETHING.
YOU CAN HAVE IT.
IF YOU GET THE DON TO SEND HIS MEN TO GET DARIO BACK. NOAH, ALL OF THEM. AND THEY BETTER TREAT DARIO NICE.
...WHAT?
PURR YOU DO SO MUCH FOR DON LORENZO. YOU DESERVE A LITTLE POWER.
...YOU HAVE NO IDEA WHAT I'VE DONE FOR HIM!
YOU'RE RIGHT.
MM-HM.
HE COULDN'T LIFT A SPOON WITHOUT ME, MUCH LESS WAGE A WAR. NO ONE KNOWS THIS FAMILY HAS BEEN MINE FOR YEARS.
GIVE ME THAT.
LORENZO, I DO NOT CARE. I HAVE A CALL TO MAKE!
ATTAGIRL.

GOTHAM.
zzrbt
AAHHHH!
just hold on
we've got you
the driving got worse, is it you
not me. possibly noah
WHAT/??
HOW IS THAT BTETER?!
BRATTATATAT
TUSCANY.
VALMONT, YOU SAID YOU HAVE A PICKUP ON THE WAY?
LUCKILY, SOME OF MY ASSOCIATES WERE CLOSE. I'M HEADING TO A NEARBY AIRSTRIP TO MEET THEM NOW.

I GET TO MEET YOUR FRIENDS?
HOW EXCITING.
THEY CERTAINLY CAN BE.
...WHAT, NO HELICOPTER?
THESE AFOREMENTIONED FRIENDS OF YOURS...
THEY'RE NOT MAKING A SPECIAL STOP FOR US--WE'RE JUST HOPPING ON A CARGO ROUTE.
AND IN MY DEFENSE...I THOUGHT WE'D BE GOING MUCH FARTHER.
SAID IT'LL BE ABOUT 45 MINUTES, MINIMUM.
I'M HAPPY YOU WERE ABLE TO GET A RIDE. AFTER ALL, I WAS WORRIED ABOUT YOUR FRIENDS IN THIS PART OF THE WORLD.
...PARDON?
WELL, IF WE'RE BEING TECHNICAL, YOU SAID YOU'D RENOUNCED KILLING POUR MOI.
FIGURED THAT SORT OF PUT YOU AT ODDS WITH THE LEAGUE OF ASSASSINS.

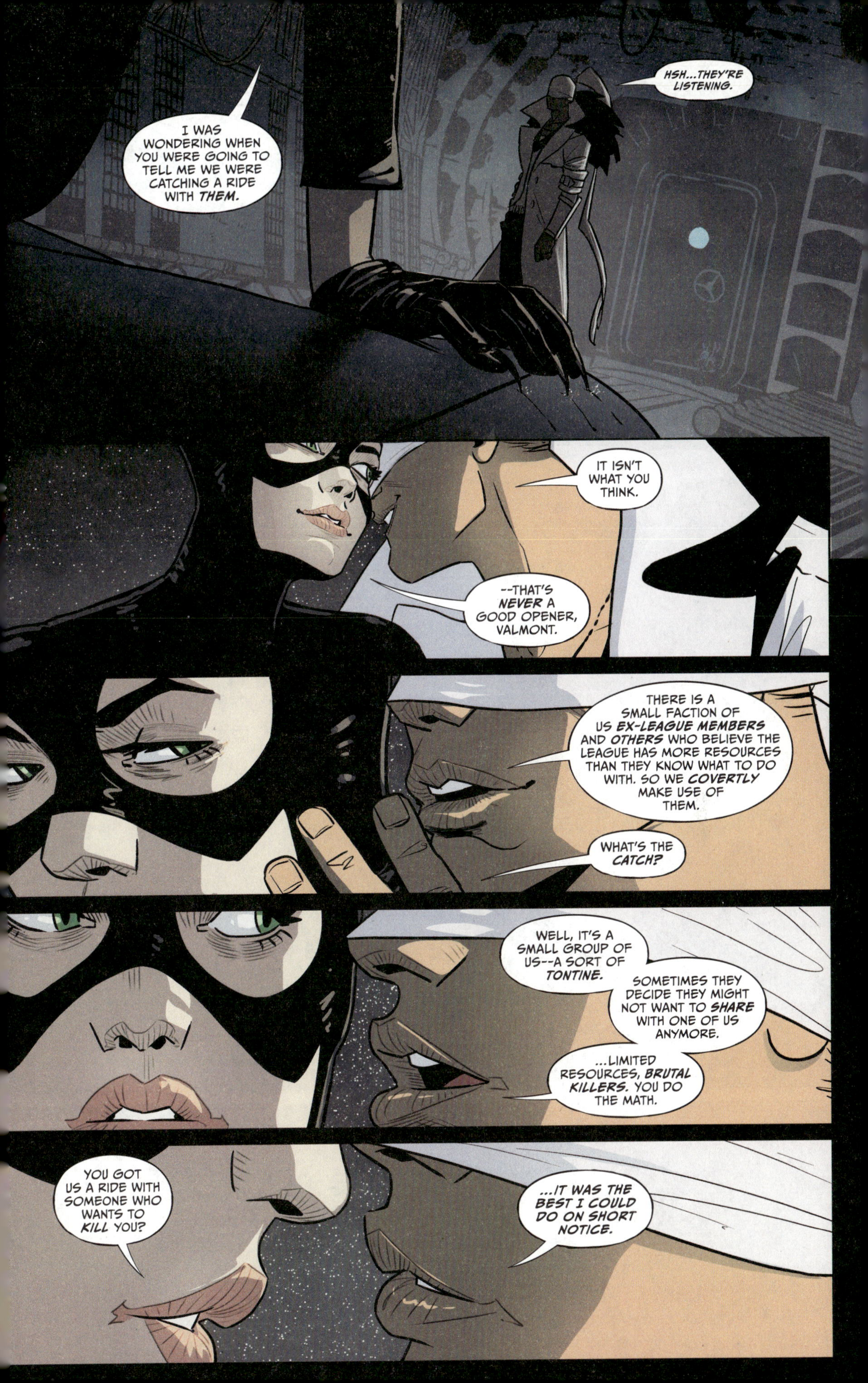
I WAS WONDERING WHEN YOU WERE GOING TO TELL ME WE WERE CATCHING A RIDE WITH *THEM.*
HSH...THEY'RE LISTENING.
IT ISN'T WHAT YOU THINK.
--THAT'S *NEVER* A GOOD OPENER, VALMONT.
THERE IS A SMALL FACTION OF US *EX-LEAGUE MEMBERS* AND *OTHERS* WHO BELIEVE THE LEAGUE HAS MORE RESOURCES THAN THEY KNOW WHAT TO DO WITH. SO WE *COVERTLY* MAKE USE OF THEM.
WHAT'S THE *CATCH?*
WELL, IT'S A SMALL GROUP OF US--A SORT OF *TONTINE.*
SOMETIMES THEY DECIDE THEY MIGHT NOT WANT TO *SHARE* WITH ONE OF US ANYMORE.
...LIMITED RESOURCES, *BRUTAL KILLERS.* YOU DO THE MATH.
YOU GOT US A RIDE WITH SOMEONE WHO WANTS TO *KILL* YOU?
...IT WAS THE BEST I COULD DO ON SHORT NOTICE.

GOOD THING I KNOW HOW TO FLY A PLANE.
I CAN AS WELL, IN A PINCH--
WE'RE NOT ALONE BACK HERE.
YOU HANDLE THE CARGO BAY AND I'LL GET THE PILOT.
I WAS JUST THINKING, I COULD USE A LITTLE SPACE.
FLAMINGO?!
¡ENCANTADO, CATWOMAN!
THAT'S HOW YOU KNOW HIM, VALMONT? YOU ALL SHARE A PLANE?!
AMONG OTHER THINGS. WE ARE AMONG THE WORLD'S FINEST KILLERS!
HE'S A CANNIBAL!
AND IF HE'S NOT GOING TO STOP ANYTIME SOON, WE'LL NEED TWO PARACHUTES--
--UNH!
WHAM!
I KNOW YOU PREFER TO EAT FACES, FLAMINGO, BUT MY HEELS WILL HAVE TO DO!

IS THAT HOW *IMPERSONAL* WE'VE BECOME?
NO NAME, NO FACE?
NOT FOR THOSE OUTSIDE OF OUR CIRCLE, OLD FRIEND.
THIS ISN'T A MISSION THAT REQUIRES FACES, VALMONT.
THIS IS AN *EXTERMINATION.* EUTHANASIA.
WE DON'T WANT TO SHARE WITH ONE WHO HAS *GIVEN UP THE KILL.*
I'LL RIP THOSE MASKS OFF AND LOOK YOU IN YOUR DYING EYES!
THOK
WE MADE THIS BOND IN *BLOOD*--AND NOW YOU HIDE FROM ME?
YOU *BELIEVE* I WON'T KILL?
THUD
BELIEVE ME NOW?
YOU MAY HAVE BEEN *BORN* TO IT, BUT THE REST OF US *EARNED* LUXURY.
AND WE'RE DONE SHARING WITH YOU!

KLIK
HOLD STILL, GATITA.
YOU IDIOT MAN, IF YOU FIRE THAT IN HERE--
BANG!!
PTING
PTING
--YOU COULD KILL US ALL!
WHY WOULDN'T I WANT TO?!
FLAMINGO, DON'T YOU--
WHAM
SSSSS
WHAT'S BETTER THAN CRASHING IN THE MOUNTAINS AND EATING YOU ALL TO SURVIVE?!

PULL UP!
PULL UP!
PULL UP!
WHANG
VALMONT!
BEEP BEEP BEEP BEEP BE
WHAT HAVE YOU DONE TO THESE CONTROLS?
YOUR BOY FLAMINGO TRASHED THE CONTROLS--PLANE'S GOING TO CRASH. WE HAVE TO GO NOW.
WHAM
GRAB THOSE TWO AND TAKE THEIR PARACHUTES!
AND THAT FACE-EATING FREAK ISN'T MY BOY.
THIS MAY HAVE BEEN A MISTAKE, VALMONT.
NO. I THREW ONE OF THEM OUT HERE WITHOUT A PARACHUTE.
THERE SHOULD BE ONE EXTRA.
I HAVE TO CONFESS--
THAT YOU KILLED SOMEONE? LOOK, IT'S A PLANE FULL OF ASSASSINS, I GET IT--
NO.

BRRRRCHKKKBRRRRRRR
I AM WILD ABOUT YOU, SELINA KYLE, ENOUGH TO MAKE ME FOOLISH. MORE THAN I HAVE EVER BEEN, FOR ANY MAN OR WOMAN.
YOU MUST FORGIVE MY LACK OF A PLAN--WHEN I FIRST CAME TO GOTHAM, I DID NOT EXPECT TO FALL FOR YOU LIKE THIS.
VALMONT...
...WHY ON EARTH ARE YOU TELLING ME THIS NOW?
BECAUSE I TRULY AM CONCERNED THAT WE MAY DIE.

AND BECAUSE I MUST BE AN HONEST GENTLEMAN ABOUT MY INTENTIONS WHEN I ASK YOU TO *WRAP YOUR LEGS AROUND ME.*
OH!
When you think you might die, everything moves slower.
When you think you might be falling for someone, everything they do feels important.
We're clinging to each other like the ground is coming up too fast.

Falling always disorients me.
fwhump
I don't always land on my feet.
gasp
NEXT: BAT'S BACK IN TOWN!

CATWOMAN #49
1:25 VARIANT COVER BY TULA LOTAY

GOTHAM CITY. NOW.
LOW BATTERY
OH MAN... C'MON, CATWOMAN... CALL BACK...I DON'T WANNA DIE IN THE TRUNK OF MY EX-BOYFRIEND'S CAR...
WHAM
HEY!
OKAY, CAT.
I'VE HUNG IN LONG ENOUGH WHILE YOU'RE ON YOUR EUROPEAN VACAY.
WHAM! WHAM!
I CAN TANGLE WITH NOAH MYSELF.

DARIO, MY DEAR?!
I'M GONNA NEED YOU TO DRIVE.
HKK-HKK-KCCH!
SCREEECH!

BRATTATATATATATA
AAAAH!
I DON'T KNOW HOW!
TO DRIVE?
...ARE YOU KIDDING ME?!
I SWEAR. FOR ALL THE POWER YOU RICH BOYS HAVE--
SQUISH
THE INCOMPETENCE YOU GET AWAY WITH IS JUST--
--STAGGERING!
SLASH!
YOU'RE CRAZY! HOW'M I SUPPOSE TO DRIVE--
YOU'RE NOT.
UNH!
CAN I SLOW DOWN FIRST--?!

BLAM! BLAM!
--AHH!
WHUD
VRRRRMM
...NOPE!
DARIO, IS THAT NOAH BEHIND US?
OH GOD, LOOKS LIKE IT!
--WHERE'S BLACK MASK?
HE WAS HERE, I HEARD HIS VOICE!
NOAH'S LIGHTING US UP--MAYBE HE SHOT ROMAN, TOO?
COULD WE BE THAT LUCKY?
BANG
TNK TNK TNK
IT'S POSSIBLE.
MEN I DON'T LIKE DESTROY EACH OTHER ALL THE TIME.
OPEN UP, DARIO.
BRATTATATTA!
ALRIGHT, YOU'RE GONNA HAVE TO LEARN TO DRIVE RIGHT NOW!
ALL I KNOW IS "TEN AND TWO!"
FORGET THAT, AND EVERYTHING ELSE YOU'VE EVER SEEN IN A MOVIE.
IF WE'RE GOING TO SURVIVE THIS, YOU'RE GONNA NEED TO TRUST YOUR GUT AND STAY WITH THE FLOW OF TRAFFIC.
CAN'T I JUST PULL OVER?!
NO! THEY HAVE MACHINE GUNS AND WE DON'T.
OUTPACING THEM IN THIS SPEEDING HUNK OF METAL IS OUR BEST DEFENSE.

DOONK HONK
VRRROOOOM
THE HIGHWAY SPLITS UP AHEAD--WE HAVE TO GET OUT OF TRAFFIC OR PEOPLE ARE GONNA DIE.
Guess I got some practice on that road trip after all...
THERE SHE IS!
DARIO! WHEN I SAY SO...
...NOW!
--GO HARD TO THE LEFT!
SCREEECH
LIKE THAT?!
PURRRRFECT.
YOU GOTTA STOP GETTING INVOLVED, CATWOMAN!
TSHHH!
WHAK!
BABY, I GO WHERE I WANT.
LITTLE MEN WITH BIG GUNS DON'T SCARE ME.
THAT GOES FOR DARIO, TOO?
THUD
BRATATATATA
I'LL BET IT DOESN'T!
AAAAAGH!

STAY UP HERE, NOAH.
KEEP RIGHT
Alleytown: 1 MILE
@#$%~! --STOP HER!
CRAZY $#%&@!
THWUD
YOUR BOSS SAYS TO STOP ME.
BUT I'M WARNING YOU NOW--
--DON'T TRY!
BEEEEEP..
WHUD
Airbags.
Great way to keep the streets safe.
PHWUMP!
Alleytown NEXT RIGHT
If we're fast enough, they'll miss the exit--those boys think they're hard, but even they think twice before rolling into Alleytown.
CRAK!
THERE, DARIO!
THE ALLEYTOWN EXIT!
Not me.
That's my home.
WHUMP WHUMP WHUMP

...PUNCHLINE AND THE ROYAL FLUSH GANG?
WHAT THE HELL HAPPENED HERE?
WHAT? IT'S ALLEYTOWN.
IT ALWAYS LOOKS LIKE @#%$.
SOMEONE CALL 9-1-1!
WHUMP WHUMP WHUMP
STAY HERE!
Hearing someone shout help in Alleytown means someone's gonna try and rob you.
Heariing "Fire!" in Alleytown means "this robber's gotten wise--people get suspicious about help."
But "call 9-1-1" is desperate. An anonymous cry for help in the night--
LET'S BLOW BEFORE THE COPS GET HERE!
I DUNNO! THEY TOOK A LOT AND SOMETIMES THIS @#$% MAKES PEOPLE CRAZY!

HEEEEHEHEEEHEE!
GKK-GKKGK-GKK!
WOOOOOOO!
AAHHH!
HA HA!
It means people are dying.
HISSS!
IT'S CATWOMAN! COPS AIN'T COMIN'!
PUNCHLINE WOULD BE SO STOKE IF WE JUST JUMPED HER ASS--
I'D BE SO STOKED FOR YOU TO TRY.
HURK!
HEY TWO OF DIAMONDS, LITTLE HELP--?
WHUD!
NEW FRIEND? I'LL TAKE BOTH YOUR JEWELS, TWO OF DIA--
YOU'RE KIDDING ME.

BILLY?! WITH THE ROYAL FLUSH GANG?!
WHAT IS THE MATTER WITH YOU? I AM SO DISAPPOINTED!
I CAN EXPLAIN!
UNNGH!
THUD
WORKING OR PUNCHLINE? COOKING DRUGS?!
DO THE OTHER STRAYS KNOW ABOUT THIS?! YOU'RE SUPPOSED TO BE KEEPING ALLEYTOWN SAFE!*
NO NO NO! PLEASE LEMME EXPLAIN, CATWOMAN!
I JUST NEEDED TO PICK UP A QUICK JOB. IT WAS LISTED AS A DELIVERY! I DIDN'T KNOW WHAT FOR, I JUST SAID YEAH.
WASN'T TILL I SHOWED UP THAT THEY SAID IT WAS A WHOLE COSTUMED THING, WHICH IS PART OF LIVING IN GOTHAM, I GUESS, BUT I ALWAYS THINK THEY'RE LAME--
WOW, BILLY, RUDE.
NOT YOU, OTHER PEOPLE!
THEY INVITED ME TO COME TO THIS... PARTY AFTERWARDS. I DIDN'T KNOW ABOUT THE PUNCHLINE STUFF OR THE X-O CRAP UNTIL I GOT HERE. I WOULD NEVER DO THAT @#$%, YOU KNOW ME.
YEAH, THAT'S WHY I WAS SURPRISED ENOUGH TO KICK YOU! IN MY LINE OF WORK, SOMETIMES YOU GET DOPPELGÄNGERS.
I'M CONTACTING LEO NOW TO MAKE SURE THERE ARE ACTUALLY AMBULANCES COMING.
*READ ABOUT BILLY AND THE ALLEYTOWN STRAYS IN CATWOMAN VOL. 6: FEAR STATE --JESS C.

WEEEOOOOOOEEE
YOU BELIEVE ME, RIGHT CATWOMAN!?
OF COURSE I DO--NOW LET'S GET OUT OF THE WAY SO THE E.M.T.s CAN HELP THESE POOR CLOWNS AND WE DON'T GET NABBED BY THE COPS.
PLEASE DON'T TELL THE OTHER STRAYS.
I WON'T.
I'M A LOCAL LIKE YOU, AND WE DON'T RAT OUT OUR OWN. BUT I NEED TO KNOW EVERYTHING YOU LEARNED ON THIS LITTLE JOB THAT NEVER HAPPENED.
PUNCHLINE'S GOT THE WHOLE ROYAL FLUSH GANG FUNDED AND ARMED.
THE DRUG IS CALLED X-O, AND AS YOU CAN SEE--IT DOESN'T GO DOWN SMOOTH. IT'S GROSS STREET STUFF, AND IT'S MAKING PEOPLE REALLY SICK.
I DIDN'T GET TO GO INSIDE, BUT I KNOW THEY'RE HANGIN' AROUND THE OLD ACE CHEMICAL BOTTLING PLANT IN ALLEYTOWN, THE SHUT-DOWN ONE.
BOTTLING AND SHIPPING PLANT HAS A DOCK. AND IF IT HAS DOCKS, IT'S UNDER THE CONTROL OF THE HASIGAWA CLAN.
LIE LOW. STAY AWAY FROM THESE GOONS AND MAKE SURE KIDS AREN'T GETTING AHOLD OF THIS X-O CRAP.
YOU'RE A GOOD KID.
BUT I'VE GOT ANOTHER WOUNDED STRAY I'VE GOT TO GET BACK TO. GIVE SHOES AND SKIDMARK MY LOVE?
AW, SURE...
I KNOW HOW TO HANDLE PUNCHLINE.

CATWOMAN'S SECRET APARTMENT, THE TRIXIE HOTEL.
BEEP
!
...S'LINA-- AH!
CAN YOU SIT UP?
THAT BULLET ONLY GRAZED YOU, DARIO, SO DON'T PLAN ON BEING SPOON-FED.
HEH. Y'KNOW, I ALSO GOT THE #@$% BEAT OUTTA ME, BUT YEAH, I CAN FEED MYSELF.
IF YOU EAT THIS WHILE I'M GONE YOU CAN HAVE A BOWL OF ICE CREAM WHEN I GET BACK.
I'D RATHER HAVE A STIFF DRINK.
NOT WITH THE PAINKILLERS YOU'RE ON.
YOU GOIN' BACK OUT? YOU GOTTA SLEEP.
NO SUCH LUCK. THERE'S A BIG GAY GOODFELLA BLEEDING IN MY BED.
HAAAH-- DON'T MAKE ME LAUGH, IT HURTS.
HA HA...HEY. LISTEN...
I'M...SO SORRY I DIDN'T GET TO YOU SOONER, DARIO. I'M GOING TO FEEL GUILTY ABOUT THAT FOR A LONG TIME.

WHY? 'CAUSE YOU WAS IN BED WITH VALMONT?!
C'MAHN. I'M HAPPY FOR YA. THERE WAS A TIME I WAS HOPING TO BEAT YOU TO IT. I'M ALIVE, AND I'M EATING PASTA IN BED. I'LL BE FINE.
THIS NOAH @#$%, NOW THAT'S GONNA BE HARDER FOR ME TO DEAL WITH. IN A WEEK OR SO, I'M NOT GONNA GIVE A DAMN ABOUT BEING LOCKED IN THE TRUNK OF A CAR.
BUT I'M STILL MAD THAT HE NEVER EVEN REALLY DUMPED ME. WE JUST WENT TO WAR. AND HE SIDED WITH MY DAD.
THAT'S HOW I KNOW WHY YOU'RE BEATING YOURSELF UP.
IT'S 'CAUSE YOU FEEL GUILTY ABOUT THAT EX OF YOURS YOU WERE TELLING ME ABOUT.
...EX SOUNDS SO...FINAL.
IT'S JUST A BREAK. I HOPE HE'S OUT MEETING PEOPLE TOO.
IT MIGHT SOUND LIKE A LIE...BUT I DO.
WHEN I THINK ABOUT B--MM. MY EX... I DON'T FEEL LIKE HE'S THE PAST I'M RUNNING FROM, I FEEL LIKE HE'S MY FUTURE.
AND I JUST HOPE THAT HE STILL WANTS WHO I AM WHEN WE GET THERE.
WELL HE BETTER.
THE SELINA KYLE I'VE COME TO KNOW AIN'T THE KIND OF WOMAN TO WAIT ON ANYONE.

LATER...
KRAK!
KRAK!
Eiko and I have an agreement--when I'm away, she plays the Cat.
--I LET YOU CATCH ME...
It's a break for us both--there are lots of things a Hasigawa crime boss can't do herself that a little alley cat can.
LIARRR!
HOW DARE YOU!
DID YOU COME TO PLAY, FELLOW CAT?
REGRETTABLY, NO--

I JUST GOT BACK, AND I ALREADY HAVE *BAD* NEWS, EIKO.
WHAT DO YOU KNOW ABOUT THE ACTIVITY AT THE ACE CHEMICAL PLANT IN ALLEYTOWN?
AH. *THAT* OLD PLACE?
IT'S LEGALLY ABANDONED, BUT I HAVE A CONTACT WHO ENSURES THAT THE DOCK REMAINS EMPTY...*UNLESS* I DECIDE THE HASIGAWA WOULD LIKE TO USE IT. WE *HAVEN'T*. THERE'S NOTHING TO IMPORT IN ALLEYTOWN.
THERE IS *NOW*.
YOUR CONTACT IS *COMPROMISED*, BECAUSE *PUNCHLINE* IS SNIFFING AROUND THERE. I THINK SHE PLANS TO USE THAT PLANT TO COOK AND SHIP DRUGS UNDER OUR NOSES.
...ALEXIS KAYE? THAT RIDICULOUS CLOWN GIRL WHO JUST GOT OUT OF PRISON?
SHE'S MADE A MISTAKE CHOOSING MY TERRITORY.
EIKO, BE CAREFUL.
I WON'T BE GOING IN MY CAT COWL. PUNCHLINE HAS CROSSED THE HASIGAWA, SO THAT IS WHO SHE'LL SEE.
BUT I *WILL* BE KEEPING THE CAT COSTUME. I *ENJOY* OUR *ARRANGEMENT*.
WE NEED A *PLAN--*
FORGIVE ME, I THOUGHT I WAS SEEING *DOUBLE*...

...I SIMPLY HAD TO GET CLOSE ENOUGH TO CHECK MY VISION.
VALMONT!
I'LL LEAVE YOU TWO ALONE.
EIKO, BE CAREFUL GOING AFTER PUNCHLINE-- DON'T BE HASTY BECAUSE YOU'RE ANGRY.
CATWOMAN... HAVE YOU SLEPT?
WHY DOES EVERYONE KEEP ASKING ME THAT?!
...HAVE YOU?
...I...HAVE NOT...
DARIO'S IN MY BED, AND I HAD TO COME TALK TO EIKO.
I HAVE A BED AT THE GOTHAM HILLMONT UNDER AN ASSUMED NAME.
YOU WOULD BE SAFE RESTING THERE, IF YOU'D LIKE.
BUT I WON'T ASSUME THAT JUST BECAUSE A CAT HAS SAT IN MY LAP ONCE, IT WILL DO SO WHENEVER I CALL.
THE HILLMONT... THAT'S ALL THE WAY ACROSS TOWN...

LATER.
I GUESS YOU'LL HAVE TO SHOW ME YOUR HOTEL ROOM LATER? THIS ROOFTOP WASN'T QUITE AS RESTFUL AS I'D HOPED.
STILL... REJUVENATING.
...I PROMISED YOU *REST.*
I HAVE TOO MUCH TO *DO.*
FOR A WOMAN KNOWN AS THE WORLD'S GREATEST *THIEF,* YOU NEVER SEEM TO STEAL A MOMENT FOR *YOURSELF.*
I'M NOT FROM THE HIGH-ROLLER WORLD LIKE YOU, HANDSOME. WHEN I SLACK OFF, PEOPLE GET HURT.

HAVE YOU EVER HAD ANYONE ENCOURAGE YOU TO CHASE YOUR DESIRES? JUST FOR THE SAKE OF YOUR OWN PLEASURE?
OR HAS WANTING THINGS ALWAYS MADE YOU FEEL LIKE A THIEF?
EVERYTHING I HAVE, I'VE HAD TO STEAL.
WHAT IS IT THAT YOU WANT? A MAN LIKE YOU HAS EVERYTHING.
I DON'T WISH TO OWN THINGS, I WISH TO EXPERIENCE THEM. I FIND JOY IN WANTING.
THE WHOLE WORLD IS AN ARRAY OF PLEASURES TO EXPERIENCE, QUESTIONS TO ANSWER, THE JOY OF SEEKING AND FINDING, WANTING AND GETTING.
IS IT PERHAPS A SELFISH PLEASURE? YES, BUT IT IS ALSO THE MOST HONEST ONE.
COME BACK, PLEASE? LAST TIME I WILL ASK.
PRR. I'M NOT USED TO BEING WITH A MAN SO COMFORTABLE WITH HIS OWN DESIRES.
MAYBE WANTING THINGS DOES MAKE ME FEEL LIKE A THIEF.
...MAYBE THAT'S WHY I LOVE IT.
GO. TO WHERE YOU ARE NEEDED.
THE SHARP PLEASURE OF WAITING UNTIL I SEE YOU AGAIN IS ENOUGH.

WHAK!
What do those stupid books call it?
A love language?
I swear I didn't set this up on purpose.
WHAK!
To you, stalking him like this looks creepy, but I promise...he does it to me, too.
I dozed off for longer than I meant to, and this just happens to be the next appointment on my schedule.

WZZ WZZZZZZ
ZZZ--
I NEED TO TALK TO YOU.
...
...I WANT TO TALK TO YOU.
Don't let the sweetness fool you.
A conversation like this is like playing chess with a master.
It's thrilling.
It's exciting.
YOU'RE ALWAYS WELCOME TO TALK TO ME, CAT.

BAT.
DO YOU WANT TO GO SOMEWHERE... WITHOUT THE MASKS?
NO. IT FEELS TOO NAKED TO TAKE THEM OFF.
I've slept next to this man naked for more nights than I can count, but it's that sense of the future again--
When next he sees my face, I want to be ready for him.
I JUST WANT YOUR BLESSING AND YOUR HELP. KEEP CLEAR OF ALLEYTOWN AND LET ME WORK?
WHY DON'T I DO YOU ONE BETTER--
I'VE GOT A LINE ON PUNCHLINE OF MY OWN, AND I DON'T WANT HER IN THERE ANY MORE THAN YOU DO. I'LL KEEP ALLEYTOWN CLEAR AND LET YOU WORK.
NO KIDS ON THIS ONE. NOT EVEN NIGHTWING, HE'S TOO RISKY WITH HIS HEART.
THIS IS GOING TO BE DANGEROUS, AND IF SOMETHING HAPPENS TO ONE OF THEM, I'LL NEVER FORGIVE MYSELF.
YOU DON'T HAVE TO TELL ME.

BUT I'M NOT YOUR *ONLY* ALLY, CATWOMAN.
AND IT SOUNDS LIKE YOU'VE GOT A BIG PLAN.
"YOU HAVE A *LOT* OF ALLIES. A LOT OF *FRIENDS*. AND A LOT OF PEOPLE WHO *TRUST* YOU.
"A LOT OF PEOPLE WHO ARE WILLING TO *FIGHT* FOR YOUR CAUSE.
"EVEN IF THEY DON'T KNOW ALL YOUR INTENTIONS, THEY TRUST YOUR *ACTIONS*.
"YOU'VE SHOWN YOURSELF TO BE A *LEADER*.
"...SO YOU'LL FIND FOLLOWERS IN UNEXPECTED PLACES."

CATWOMAN
FURIOUS HEARTS PART 2 OF
TINI HOWARD STORY NICO LEON
VERONICA GANDINI COLORS LUCAS GATTONI
JEFF DÉKAL COVER SOZOMAIKA
TULA LOTAY 1:25 VARIANT
JIM BALENT '90s REWIND VARIANT
JESSICA BERBEY ASSISTANT
JESSICA CHEN
BEN ABERNATHY GROUP
AND YOU?
WILL YOU FOLLOW MY LEAD ON THIS ONE?
I WILL.
I ALWAYS TRUST YOU TO GET THE JOB DONE.
"NO MATTER WHAT SURPRISES GET THROWN YOUR WAY."
"Oh Bat, you know me...
"I'm hard to surprise."
NEXT: A CAT, A CROW, AND THEIR CREW

UTION POLI
T CROS

CATWOMAN #50
1:25 VARIANT COVER BY **TULA LOTAY**

THE ACE CHEMICALS PLANT HAS BEEN UNDER HASIGAWA CONTROL, BUT PUNCHLINE AND HER ROYAL FLUSH GANG HAVE BEEN WAITING TO POUNCE.
THE PLANT'S BEEN ABANDONED SINCE THE '90s. IT'S AN ARTIFACT OF THEIR BRIEF FORAY INTO ENERGY DRINKS.
HEMORRHAGE? I USED TO DRINK THOSE!
THAT EXPLAINS A LOT.
CATWOMAN'S APARTMENT, THE TRIXIE, GOTHAM CITY.
OUR MISSION IS TO DESTROY THEIR LITTLE SHOP SO BADLY THEY LIMP AWAY.
PUNCTURE CANISTERS, CONTROLLED DEMOLITIONS OF LABS, BLOODY THE NOSES OF THE ROYAL FLUSH GANG--AND NOT A BIT OF IT GETS OUT INTO ALLEYTOWN.
ROYAL FLUSH GANG? THOSE PLAYING CARD LOSERS?
YEP. BUT THERE ARE 52 OF THEM, GIVE OR TAKE A FEW JOKERS, SO WE'LL HAVE TO BE SMART ABOUT IT.
BILLY AND THE STRAYS ARE PLUGGED IN NOW--A BUNCH OF THE ROYAL FLUSH GANG LOW NUMBERS JUST GOT RELEASED FROM THEIR SHIFTS--
"--AND THEY'RE BEING HANDLED.
"DARIO, YOU'LL BE IN CONTACT WITH LEO ON THEIR TEAM, LINKING EVERYONE UP."
WE'LL GET YOU CLOSER TO THE ACTION, BUT BE CAREFUL--YOU'RE STILL HEALING.
ONYX, I HAVE YOU WITH VALMONT UNTIL WE LINK UP. YOU'LL BE HANDLING THE GENERALS--LUCKY FOR US, THEY'RE DUMB ENOUGH TO MARK THEMSELVES WITH FACE CARDS.
I'LL BE ALONE MOST OF IT, BUT I'LL HAVE EIKO WATCHING MY BACK, IF SHE EVER SHOWS UP--
I CAN WATCH YOUR BACK.

CAT. I NEED TO TALK TO YOU...
ALONE.
CATWOMAN
FURIOUS HEARTS
PART 3 OF
TINI HOWARD
NICO LEON
VERONICA GANDINI
LUCAS GATTONI
DAVID NAKAYAMA
SOZOMAIKA VARIANT AND 1:50 FOIL VARIANT
STJEPAN ŠEJIĆ VARIANT
TULA LOTAY 1:25 VARIANT
NATHAN SZERDY HOLIDAY VARIANT
DAVID MARQUEZ SPAWN VARIANT
JESSICA BERBEY ASSISTANT
JESSICA CHEN
BEN ABERNATHY GROUP

BAT.
IF YOU'RE GOING TO HELP, I NEED YOU INSIDE. I DON'T APPRECIATE THE INTERRUPTION.
IT'S EIKO.
I JUST TOOK HER TO THE HOSPITAL.*
*SEE PUNCHLINE #2 FOR WHAT HAPPENED TO EIKO! --JESS C.
WHAT?
PUNCHLINE AND EIKO FOUGHT AT THE CHEMICAL PLANT.
THEY GOT INTO A KNIFE FIGHT AT CLOSE RANGE...
...I HAD TO INTERFERE. SHE WOULD HAVE KILLED PUNCHLINE.
WHAT?
I WAS NOT GOING TO LET HER COMMIT A MURDER IN FRONT OF ME, CAT. NOT EVEN PUNCHLINE.
EIKO GOT STABBED, AND TOOK A FALL--
WHICH HOSPITAL--!?
SHE'S NOT EVEN AWAKE, CAT. SHE'S HURT BADLY.

YOU HAVE WORK TO DO.
AND I'M HERE FOLLOWING YOUR ORDERS. LIKE I PROMISED.
BAT... THE TEMPERATURE AROUND HERE IS BOILING LATELY. THIS WON'T STOP UNTIL SOMEONE'S DEAD.
WE'RE NOT LETTING ANYONE DIE.
SOUNDS LIKE YOU'RE GIVING ME ORDERS.
I WOULDN' DARE.
EIKO WILL NEED YOU A SOON AS YO CAN BE THER WHETHER SHE AWAKE OR NOT.
BUT ALLEYTOWN NEEDS ME NOW.
THIS CITY ALWAYS WILL.
...NO ONE UNDERSTANDS THAT LIKE YOU, BAT.
MM.
LEAD THE WAY.

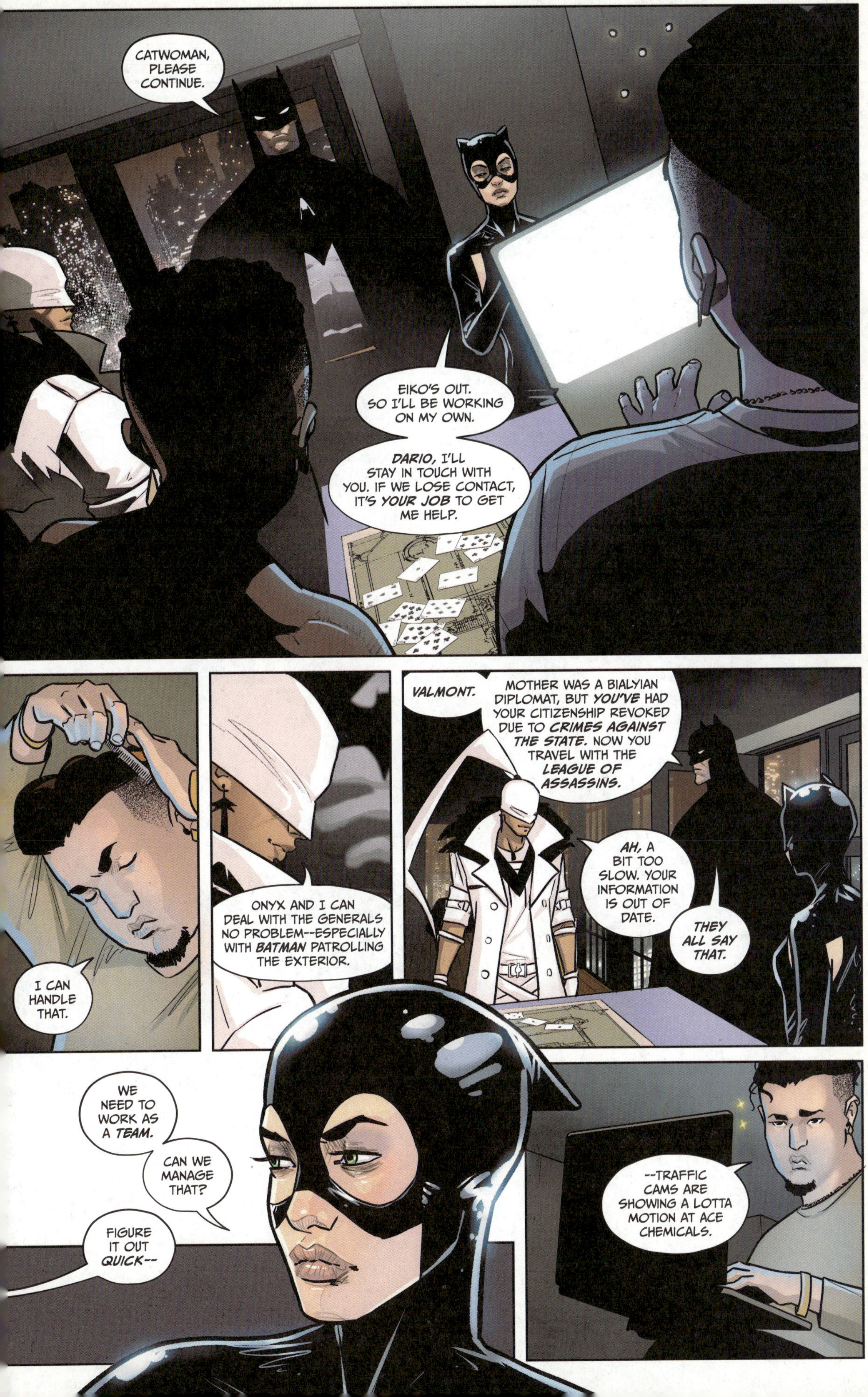
CATWOMAN, PLEASE CONTINUE.
EIKO'S OUT. SO I'LL BE WORKING ON MY OWN.
DARIO, I'LL STAY IN TOUCH WITH YOU. IF WE LOSE CONTACT, IT'S *YOUR JOB* TO GET ME HELP.
I CAN HANDLE THAT.
ONYX AND I CAN DEAL WITH THE GENERALS NO PROBLEM--ESPECIALLY WITH *BATMAN* PATROLLING THE EXTERIOR.
VALMONT.
MOTHER WAS A BIALYIAN DIPLOMAT, BUT *YOU'VE* HAD YOUR CITIZENSHIP REVOKED DUE TO *CRIMES AGAINST THE STATE.* NOW YOU TRAVEL WITH THE *LEAGUE OF ASSASSINS.*
AH, A BIT TOO SLOW. YOUR INFORMATION IS OUT OF DATE.
THEY ALL SAY THAT.
WE NEED TO WORK AS A *TEAM.*
CAN WE MANAGE THAT?
FIGURE IT OUT *QUICK--*
--TRAFFIC CAMS ARE SHOWING A LOTTA MOTION AT ACE CHEMICALS.

ACE CHEMICALS
GET TO WORK, SCRUBS!
NOW THAT WE'VE GOT ACCESS TO ACE CHEMICALS PLANT, PRODUCTION OF X-O NEEDS TO RAMP UP FAST. WE'VE ALREADY GOT THE KIDS OF ALLEYTOWN HOOKED, AND IF WE CAN KEEP UP DEMAND, WE'LL BUST OUT INTO THE REST OF GOTHAM.
I DIDN'T COME OUT OF RETIREMENT TO STUFF ENVELOPES, PUNCHLINE, AND NEITHER DID MY WIFE.
IT WOULD GO A LOT FASTER IF EVERYONE WOULD HELP WITH THE BUSYWORK--
YEAH, YOU TWO ARE JUST HERE TO STUFF PUNCHLI--
HEY! SHUT THE @#$% UP! THIS ISN'T A JOKE.
I LIKE WHAT I'VE DONE HERE, AND THAT MEANS BEING READY TO DEFEND IT. CATWOMAN THINKS SHE'S GOT A HOLD ON ANY AND ALL ORGANIZED CRIME IN GOTHAM? SHE THINKS SHE CAN USE THEIR RULES AGAINST THEM?
WELL WHAT IF I DON'T HAVE RULES, @#$%%-- WHAT THEN?
THAT'S JUST PART OF WHY WE WORK SO WELL TOGETHER. MY QUEEN OF HEARTS AND I ARE JUST HERE TO HAVE A GREAT TIME.
THERE'S ONLY ONE THING MY KING AND I LOVE MORE THAN A FIGHT, AND THAT'S MEANT FOR LATER.

WE SURE AREN'T ORGANIZED AND WE'RE NOT TECHNICALLY CRIME. THEY HAVEN'T FIGURED OUT WHAT TO DO WITH US.
JUST LIKE YOU HAVEN'T FIGURED OUT WHAT TO DO WITH US, PUNCHLINE?
WHUMP
I'M TEMPTED TO PUT YOU ON JANITORIAL DUTY FOR THAT COMMENT, JACK.
OWW, OKAY, FINE, I'LL PACK SHIPMENTS OR WHATEVER!
HEAR THAT?
BRRRBRRRRRRBRRRRR
YOU FOUR MAY HAVE JUST GOT A LUCKY HAND.
RBRRRRRRRRBRRRRR
CALL ME PARANOID, BUT PUTTING HASIGAWA IN THE HOSPITAL JUST MAKES ME MORE NERVOUS HER DUDES WILL RETALIATE.
KING, QUEEN? I WANT YOU PATROLLING THE PLACE. NO MERCY. YOU DON'T RECOGNIZE SOMEONE, YOU GIVE 'EM HELL.
1-0? YOU TAKE ACES TO THE ROOF AND SCAN THE PLACE. I DON'T WANNA SEE ANY NEON DEMONS...OR ANY OTHER INVADERS.
NO BIRDS, NO BATS, AND DEFINITELY NO CATS.

SETTING UP TRIP WIRES.
PAGING FOUR OF SPADES?
I DON'T SEE ANYTHING.
I GET WHY PUNCHLINE WANTS THE WIRES SET UP, BUT LIKE...I DON'T THINK A BUNCH OF THE CAT'S CREW ARE GONNA BE TAKING THE **MAIN ROADS** TO GET IN HERE--
HK
UH... "DON'T QUESTION IT. I, UH...*GOTTA*
"I GOTTA POOP. BYE NOW!"
SKIDS, WHY YOU GOTTA--
BILLY-- SHH!
--THIS IS FOUR OF SPADES! HJK--
OOF--

WE HAVE A BREACH!
THEY'VE GOT BACKUP, ROYAL FLUSH GANG--DON'T HOLD BACK!
HEIST TEAM, WE'RE IN. GOOD JOB KEEPING THEM OFF THE ENTRANCE.
NOW, SCATTER, KITTENS.
PAGING LEO! DARIO! ONE A' YOU GUYS LET BATMAN KNOW WE COULD USE SOME HELP DOWN HERE!
I THINK UNCHLINE'S CREW OCKED A BUNCH OF Y DEVICES AT MY ACE--I'M SEEING IF GETTING CLOSER HELPS!
DOES ONE OF YOU GADGET NERDS HAVE LIKE A... LASER DRONE... OR...?
KZZSHH-- TRY--HEAR!
WE'RE NOT EVEN GETTING THROUGH!
KSHH-- CAT!
I'M NOT GONNA HANG BACK ON MY PHONE WHILE PEOPLE DIE--
HA! THEY'RE JUST KITTENS.
KNOCK 'EM OUT AND THROW 'EM IN THE WATER. CATS LOVE THAT!
LEO'S NOT RESPONDING EITHER! AND I CAN'T KEEP TRYING--WE'RE GONNA HAVE TO FOCUS TO TAKE THESE GUYS OUT.
THEN LET'S FOCUS UP!
KZZZZ
KZZZZ
KZZZZ
AAAGH!
UH!
KZZZZZ
GAAH!
SORRY, WE'RE UNEXPECTEDLY DOWN A CAT--
--AND WHILE USUALLY I'M AN INDOOR ONE, IF MY PACK NEEDS ME--

--OUT HERE, CALL ME TOMCAT.

BIG CAT'S NOT GONNA LIKE THIS. SHE'S WEIRD ABOUT SIDEKICKS. I WOULD KNOW.
I AIN'T A SIDEKICK.
YOU MUST BE SHOES?
WE NEEDED ANOTHER CAT.
WHOOSH
THAT'S WHY I'M HERE. NICE TO MEET YOU. I'M CHESHIRE CAT, MOST DAYS.
CATWOMAN AID SHE DOESN'T WANT ANY MORE NOCENTS JOINING HIS WAR, BUT I'M IN THIS LIFE BY BLOOD.
PUTTING ON A MASK IS THE BEST I CAN DO.
WE HAVE THAT IN COMMON.
ONE MORE THING YOU CAN DO?
OF!
LET YOUR LEGS HELP IN THE PUNCH, TOO.
FREE TIP FROM A FELLOW VIGILANTE.
LET'S GET THESE GUYS TIED AND TRY TO FIX THE COMMS--THERE'S PROBABLY AN ON-SITE JAMMER.
SURE THING. AND HEY, I KNOW THEY SAY CATS ARE LONERS, BUT...
IT'S NOT TRUE.
WELCOME TO THE FAMILY, TOMCAT.

COME IN, TEAM--?
PUNCHLINE JAMMED THE COMMS. SHE KNEW WHOEVER WAS COMING AFTER HER WAS GOING TO BRING A TEAM--
HEEEEEERE KITTY.
HEEEEEERE KITTY.
TSSSS
She's trying to gas me out, but it's just giving away her location.
Roughly. I can't quite suss out where she is to get the drop--
PUNCHLINE! THERE YOU ARE!
IT'S CATWOMAN, SHE'S INSIDE.
NO @#$%, WHAT DO YOU THINK I'M--
WAIT, LOOK--SHE'S IN THE VENT, RIGHT BEHIND YOU--

GOT HER!
CASEY, OU IDIOT, NO!
ZZZAAAAARRRK
THERE YOU ARE! THANK YOUR NEW MAN FOR ME.
I'M NOT HER M--
HE'S NOT A MAN!
HE'S A STUPID BOY, AND HE'S ABOUT TO BE THE LAST ONE YOU SEE IN YOUR WHOLE LIFE, YOU TRASHY OLD #@$^%!
AK
YOU KNOW WHAT KIND OF WOMEN CALL OTHER GIRLS OLD LIKE IT'S A BAD THING?
WHAM
...SCARED ONES.
I'M NOT SCARED OF YOU. I'D SAY YOU MAKE ME LAUGH, BUT WOMEN LIKE YOU ARE NEVER FUNNY.
NOT HERE TO MAKE YOUR DAY, ALEXIS.
HELLO? HELLO? CATWOMAN!

HELLO? DID WE FIX THE COMMS? CAN ANYONE HEAR US?
I CAN HEAR YOU. WE'RE JUST WRAPPING UP SOME INTEL GATHERING NOW.
...SECOND FLOOR...GUY NAMED KING...
AAH!
YOU CAN'T KEEP ALLEYTOWN IN YOUR POCKET JUST 'CAUSE YOU'RE SENTIMENTAL, CATWOMAN. ADMIT IT--YOU DON'T WANNA LIVE IN THESE NEIGHBORHOODS EITHER.
KSH
COME IN, CATWOMAN-- WHAT'S YOUR TWENTY?
DOES ANYONE HAVE EYES ON CATWOMAN?!
I'M ALIVE-- I'M WITH PUNCHLINE--! STAY FOCUSED ON THE MISSION!
AUTHORIZED PERSONNEL ONLY
AVEC PLAISIR.
THERE IS MUCH TO BE DONE OUT OF SIGHT.

VALMONT'S ON HIS WAY, CAT--I'M THE LOOKOUT FOR THE KING AND QUEEN OF HEARTS--TWO OF PUNCHLINE'S TOP GENERALS.
YOU'RE LOOKING FOR US?
I THINK THAT'S EXCITING.
NOW THAT WE KNOW WE LIKE EACH OTHER, ENOUGH SMALL TALK. LET'S PLAY.
GOONS PLAY. I DIDN'T COME BACK TO GOTHAM TO PLAY.
CAN WE CHANGE YOUR MIND?
UNGH--
THE LONGER I LIVE HERE THE MORE I'M SURE--EVERYONE IN GOTHAM IS A FREAK!
YOU WATCH IT--THAT FREAK IS MY HUSBAND!
KZZZTT
AAH!

WHAT DO WE HAVE HERE?
AARON HELZINGER. SIR. NOW IS THIS ANY KIND OF TREATMENT FOR A GENTLEMAN?
RRRR...
AS I IMAGINE YOU'RE HERE AS A REPRESENTATIVE OF THE GENTLEMAN'S CLUB, YES?
CATWOMAN, THEY HAVE AMYGDALA.
WHERE? CAPTURED? WHATEVER YOU DO, DON'T--
CLIK
I CAN'T LEAVE YOU IMPRISONED LIKE THIS... IT WOULDN'T BE RIGHT. IT'S NOT FAIR OF SOMEONE LIKE PUNCHLINE TO THINK SOMEONE LIKE YOU IS...
...UNPREDICTABLE.
THIS WAY... LOOK HERE!
ARE YOU MAD AT PUNCHLINE? WANT TO DO SOMETHING ABOUT IT?
RRRH-RGHH--RAAHHH--!

NEVER MIND.
I DON'T THINK SHE'S CUTE ANYMORE.
ME NEITHER. SHE DROPPED LIKE A SACK OF POTATOES.
I NEED A LOVER WHO CAN TAKE A *LITTLE* ELECTRICITY AT *LEAST*.
I THINK THAT'S FAIR--
THINK I'M CUTE *NOW?*
SLASH
AHH!!
THAT'S FROM THE *CAT*--
THIS ONE'S FROM *ME*--
WHUD
--JUST SO YOU LEARN TO GET BETTER.
GENERALS *DOWN*.
PRETTY SURE I'VE SEEN THESE TWO BEFORE--BUT THEY'RE *RUSTY*. MUST'VE COME OUT OF RETIREMENT.
STATUS?

ACCK!
THOK!
I'M HERE.
I'M HANDLING PUNCHLINE. I NEED THE AREA CLEARED--WE'VE GOT A BUNCH OF THIS X-O IN THE VENTS, AND THERE'S EVERY INDICATION IT'S FLAMMABLE IN THESE PRESSURIZED CONTAINERS.
THIS IS TOMCAT. WE'RE CLEAR. NO ONE'S AROUND TO BREATHE THIS CRAP IF WE RELEASE IT.
OVER.
THIS IS WHO?!
CAN'T EVEN KEEP TRACK OF YOUR OWN KIDS? JUST LIKE A CAT.
WE'LL TALK ABOUT THIS LATER.
ALEXIS KAYE, THIS STOPS NOW.

I'M NOT A FAN OF LOCKING PEOPLE UP AND THROWING AWAY THE KEY, BUT FOR YOU, I'D SWALLOW THAT KEY MYSELF.
WELL, I'D--HNNG-- ENJOY CUTTING YOU OPEN TO GET IT BACK.
YOU'LL CERTAINLY HAVE TIME TO FANTASIZE ABOUT THAT IN PRISON.
KKKH-- HEH--LITTLE TIGHT THERE, KILLER-- KOFF
YOU'LL BE FINE--
CATWOMAN! IT'S AMYGDALA, HE'S--
AARRGGHHH!

KILL KITTY!
YOU STUPID-ASS
KOFF
LET GO OF ME!
KILL--AH!
RIIIIIP
YOU MONSTER! YOU KILLED HIM!
AND I'LL KILL YOU, TOO, IF YOU DON'T PACK UP AND MOVE, LITTLE GIRL.
YOU'RE CRAZY. HE'S CRAZY.
VALMONT...
...YOU PROMISED YOU WOULD STOP KILLING FOR ME. YOU PROMISED...

DID ONE
F THE CLOWN'S
NIVES GET YOU, LOVER?
MA TIGRESSE, I'LL KILL HER SLOW--
KILLER.
NOT IN MY CITY.
BAT-- NO!
YOUR CITY? AND WHO GAVE IT TO YOU?
HE NEEDS TO
DO TIME, CAT! AMYGDALA IS DEAD.
YOUR HANDS ARE CLEAN.
NOT IF YOU WALK FREE!
EVENTUALLY YOU WILL LEARN THE PRICE OF PROTECTING THOSE YOU LOVE.
MAN OF THE WORLD? MAN OF THE LEAGUE.
--AND I KNOW A DEEP-COVER MISSION WHEN I SEE ONE.
SAY WHAT YOU MEAN.
I WOULDN'T DO THAT TO HER--

KRAK!
STOP--
SHHHINK
There's too much blood for this fight.
WHAP
THWAM
CREEAAAAKKK--
WHAMMM
HNGHH--
I'VE GOT YOU.
They don't see it yet--

--but I do.
Do you trust me?
SHHTHKK!

He does.
Even now, at the end, he tells me--
CAT-- WE NEED TO MOVE--
all I can think...
...to the very end.

THE NEXT DAY.
GOOD MORNING. THANK YOU ALL FOR COMING.
WE'RE HERE TO ADDRESS THIS MORNING'S ARREST IN COLLABORATION WITH THE GOTHAM CITY POLICE DEPARTMENT. THE DISTRICT ATTORNEY COULDN'T BE HERE TODAY BUT SENDS HIS REGARDS.
THIS MORNING, AT APPROXIMATELY 5:45 A.M., AN ARREST WAS MADE AT THE ALLEYTOWN LOCATION OF THE FORMER ACE CHEMICALS.
THE ARREST WAS FOR, AMONG OTHER CHARGES, ONE COUNT OF FELONY MURDER, CENTERED ON AN INDIVIDUAL WHOSE IDENTITY AND ALIAS WE WILL NOT CURRENTLY DIVULGE.
HER ACTIONS LED TO THE DEATH OF AT LEAST ONE OF HER ACCOMPLICES, WHOSE IDENTITY IS NOT BEING RELEASED AT THIS TIME.
COMMISSIONER MONTOYA! IS IT TRUE THAT CATWOMAN AND BATMAN WERE ALSO PRESENT AT THE SCENE?!
IS THE GCPD RETURNING TO A POLICY OF TAKING VIGILANTES INTO CUSTODY?
IS IT TRUE THAT ALEXIS KAYE WAS PRESENT ON THE SCENE?!
THE SUSPECT IS ALSO BEING LINKED TO SEVERAL EXPLOSIVE CHEMICAL REACTIONS AT THE PLANT, DAMAGING CITY PROPERTY AND REQUIRING EVACUATION OF PARTS OF ALLEYTOWN.
ARE THERE PLANS TO INVESTIGATE THE COSTUMED CRIMINAL KNOWN AS PUNCHLINE?!

PART II:

"THE AFTERMATH"

TINI HOWARD writer INAKI MIRANDA (pgs. 1-6) & JUAN FERREYRA artists (pgs. 7-16)

JUAN FERREYRA & LEE LOUGHRIDGE colorists DERON BENNETT letterer

JESSICA BERBEY assistant editor JESSICA CHEN editor

"DAMN... I WAS KINDA PISSED WHEN YOU DIDN'T SHOW UP FOR SELINA'S BIG MISSION, BUT BATMAN WASN'T KIDDING...
...PUNCHLINE GOT YOU GOOD, EIKO.
NOT GOOD ENOUGH. SHE'LL REGRET IT...
...OR DOES SHE ALREADY? I GATHER FROM YOUR EXPRESSION, DARIO, THAT SOMETHING HAS GONE... POORLY.
SOME OF THE ALLEYTOWN KIDS AND I GOT EVERYONE OUT BEFORE THE EXPLOSION, BUT THE AREA'S A MESS.
THE PLANT IS TRASHED. NO ONE'S GOING TO BE SHIPPING ANYTHING OUT OF THERE FOR A LONG TIME.
THAT'S GOOD, ISN'T IT?
DON'T HOLD BACK. I NEED TO KNOW.

SELINA'S IN CUSTODY. VALMONT'S... *DEAD.*
WHAT? *HOW?!* THEY ARRESTED SELINA FOR *PUNCHLINE'S* OPERATION?!
VALMONT KILLED AMYGDALA. THE BAT TURNED ON VALMONT.
SELINA GOT BETWEEN THEM--
THEY THINK SHE DID IT?!
...*SHE* THINKS SHE DID IT, EIKO.
I'M SUPPOSED TO WATCH HER APARTMENT...FEED HER CAT WHILE SHE'S BEHIND BARS.
BEEP BEEP BEEP BEEP
EIKO, WHAT ARE YOU DOING?!
COME. TALK TO ME, DARIO.

WHY ARE YOU STANDING? WHY ARE YOU HERE, EIKO?
WOULDN'T IT BE BETTER FOR YOU TO HEAL UP OUTTA TOWN? GET THE @#$% OUT OF GOTHAM AND LET YOUR BOYS RULE THE STREETS?
ABANDON MY TERRITORY? WEAK. I THINK PERHAPS YOUR FATHER IS RIGHT ABOUT ONE THING, DARIO...
YOU AREN'T MADE FOR CRIMINAL LEADERSHIP.
BUT YOU HAVE OTHER SKILLS. SPEAKING OF WHICH... I HAVE OTHER EARS IN ALLEYTOWN.
I'VE HEARD ABOUT YOUR RECENT TURN AS THE TOMCAT.
CATS AREN'T PACK ANIMALS. GIVE ME ONE GOOD REASON NOT TO PUT ON MY SUIT AND RUN YOU OUT OF TOWN--AGH--
HOW'S THAT, FOR ONE.
MMMNGNH-- DAMN.
AND YOU SAY SELINA'S LIKELY TO BE AWAY FOR SOME TIME?
YEAH. AT LEAST TILL SHE GETS A TRIAL.

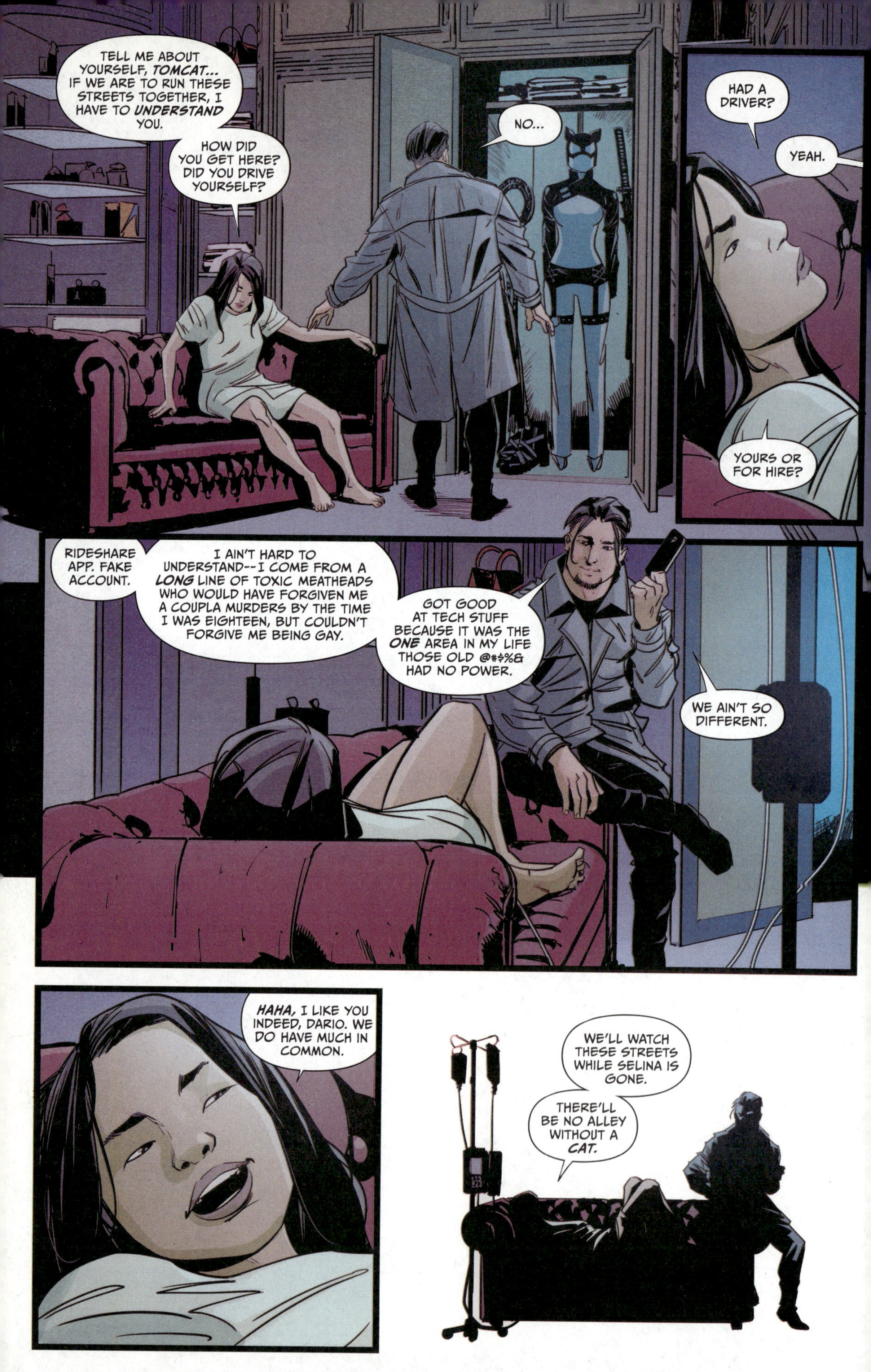

TELL ME ABOUT YOURSELF, TOMCAT... IF WE ARE TO RUN THESE STREETS TOGETHER, I HAVE TO UNDERSTAND YOU.
HOW DID YOU GET HERE? DID YOU DRIVE YOURSELF?
NO...
HAD A DRIVER?
YEAH.
YOURS OR FOR HIRE?
RIDESHARE APP. FAKE ACCOUNT.
I AIN'T HARD TO UNDERSTAND--I COME FROM A LONG LINE OF TOXIC MEATHEADS WHO WOULD HAVE FORGIVEN ME A COUPLA MURDERS BY THE TIME I WAS EIGHTEEN, BUT COULDN'T FORGIVE ME BEING GAY.
GOT GOOD AT TECH STUFF BECAUSE IT WAS THE ONE AREA IN MY LIFE THOSE OLD @#$%& HAD NO POWER.
WE AIN'T SO DIFFERENT.
HAHA, I LIKE YOU INDEED, DARIO. WE DO HAVE MUCH IN COMMON.
WE'LL WATCH THESE STREETS WHILE SELINA IS GONE.
THERE'LL BE NO ALLEY WITHOUT A CAT.

GOTHAM COUNTY JAIL. NOW.
BZZZZZT
WE'RE RIGHT OUTSIDE IF YOU NEED US, MR. WAYNE.
C'MON, GIVE THE GUY SOME PRIVACY.
CHK

HELLO, BRUCE.
THANK YOU FOR THE VISIT. I HOPE THEY DIDN'T MAKE YOU WAIT TOO LONG WHILE THEY CAVITY SEARCHED ME.
THEY DON'T MAKE ME WAIT.
I HAD TO STOP AND VISIT MY LAWYERS BEFORE I ARRIVED HERE.
DON'T WORRY, NO ONE'S GOING TO MAKE YOU TESTIFY.
I WASN'T ASKING THEM ABOUT ME, SELINA. THE LEGAL SYSTEM IN GOTHAM ISN'T SOMETHING I WOULD WISH ON MY WORST ENEMY, MUCH LESS YOU.
JUST TO PLEAD GUILTY, YOU'LL NEED A GOOD LEGAL TEAM TO PROTECT YOU FROM ABUSE.
SELINA...
...WHY DID YOU DO IT?
TO SAVE YOUR LIFE--
YOU DIDN'T NEED TO--
YOU DON'T TRUST MY JUDGMENT. YOUR EGO DOESN'T LIKE IT.
YOU THINK HE COULDN'T HAVE KILLED THE GREAT BATMAN.
I WAS SO AFRAID OF WHAT WOULD HAPPEN IF I HAD TO CHOOSE BETWEEN YOU.
NOW THAT IT'S HAPPENED, ALL I CAN THINK ABOUT... IS ALLEYTOWN.
I FAILED THIS CITY, BRUCE.
I THOUGHT NO ONE WOULD UNDERSTAND THAT LIKE YOU.

I WOULD RATHER HAVE LET HIM TRY, SELINA. I AM NOT AFRAID TO DIE--I AM AFRAID OF--
WHAT, BRUCE?
SEEING ME SUFFER? ARE YOU AFRAID OF LOVING PEOPLE WHO BECOME THINGS YOU DON'T RECOGNIZE? ARE YOU AFRAID OF WHAT HAPPENS WHEN WE TRUST OUR OWN JUDGMENT INSTEAD OF YOURS?
LOOK, I GOT A LOT WRONG LAST NIGHT.
I DIDN'T KNOW AMYGDALA WAS THERE. I @#$%~& UP. HE'S DEAD BECAUSE I TRUSTED VALMONT. PUNCHLINE GOT AWAY LAUGHING BECAUSE I GOT THINGS WRONG.
BUT I KNOW WHAT I SAW. I DON'T REGRET A THING.
SELINA, IF WE'RE ADMITTING TO UNCOMFORTABLE TRUTHS...
...I COULD NEVER FAULT YOU FOR FALLING FOR A KILLER. SOMETIMES... I THINK--
--YOU AND I ARE SOME OF THE LAST ONES WHO REALLY DON'T WANT TO BE KILLERS. IN A WORLD LIKE THIS, THAT MEANS SOMETHING.
...I WISH WE WERE HAVING THIS CONVERSATION ANYWHERE ELSE RIGHT NOW.

YOU AND I HAVE BEEN TO HELL AND BACK. ANYTHING IN BETWEEN IS--
DON'T SAY "NOTHING."
DON'T SAY HE WAS NOTHING.
...I WOULD NEVER.
NO LIFE IS.
LOOK AT US. MASKS OFF. HAVING THE HARD CONVERSATIONS.
IT ONLY TOOK ME HITTING ROCK BOTTOM.
I LOVE YOU, BRUCE. I ALWAYS WILL.
I LOVE YOU, SELINA.
WE'LL SEE ABOUT THAT.
HOW MANY NIGHTS ARE YOU GOING TO SHUT YOUR EYES AND SEE ME KILLING, EVEN IF IT WAS TO SAVE YOU?
BZZT
I HAVE TO GO.
YOU KNOW, I AM CAPABLE OF FORGIVENESS, SELINA.
LET ME FORGIVE MYSELF FIRST.

GOTHAM COUNTY JAIL COMMON AREA.
BZZZT
SH-THUNK
LADIES! FRESH CATCH!
SELINA KYLE, EVERYONE! SHE USED TO BE A BIT OF A FREQUENT FLYER ROUND THE COUNTY JAIL ONCE UPON A TIME, BUT IT'S BEEN A MINUTE SINCE SHE GRACED US WITH HER PRESENCE.
WE'VE ONLY INSTALLED MORE CAMERAS AROUND HERE SINCE YOU WERE A KID, SO YOU'LL JUST HAVE TO GET SMARTER.
HEEERE FISHY FISHY FISHY--
...DON'T WANT TO FIGHT.
WHAT'S THAT, LITTLE @#$%#@? YOU DON'T WANT TO FIGHT?
NO...
I SAID YOU DON'T!
SWISH
IT'D BE THE BIGGEST MISTAKE OF YOUR LIFE, AND THAT'S SAYING A LOT, HONEY, 'CAUSE YOU'RE HERE.
SO'RE YOU.

I've been in here before--and this is my least favorite part.
It's easy to get so caught up in the system here that you just give up and get comfortable, waiting for the asses you want to kick to end up back inside.
HB 35
HB 35
It doesn't help that they don't know I'm Catwoman, actually.
But they have debts they want to take out of my bones.
And I'm feeling just dark enough to let 'em try.
Gotta make sure I miss.
I'm looking for a time-out, not extra charges.

Selina Kyle has sticky enough fingers on her own to have made a dozen enemies.
You'd think they'd leave me alone.
Felony murder.
I'm a killer.
After all, there aren't a lot of ways to get a little peace and quiet in this joint--
C'MON, GIRLS--
KRAK
--HERE'S THAT ATTENTION YOU ORDERED--
--you gotta take your chances to show off as soon as you can.
KYLE! STAND DOWN!
SOK
THUD
But I can't go down easy.
It's like gambling--gotta know when to fold so people don't think you're just a little pussycat.

SLAM
WE'LL CHECK IN ON YOU IN 72 HOURS, KYLE.
WHY DON'T YOU DO SOME THINKIN' ABOUT HOW YOU GOT HERE?
...MAGGIE ALWAYS SAID TO PRAY AT TIMES LIKE THESE.
MY GOD...
I AM SORRY FOR HAVING OFFENDED THEE... UGH.
I DON'T REMEMBER THE REST.
IT HAS BEEN A VERY LONG TIME SINCE MY LAST CONFESSION.

I DON'T HAVE ANYTHING TO SAY FOR MYSELF. I'M A SINNER AND A KILLER. I FAILED THE PEOPLE I WAS TRYING TO SAVE, AND I ASK FOR NO MERCY.
BUT PLEASE LOOK AFTER THE ONES I LOVE?
PLEASE MAKE SURE... SOMEONE FEEDS MY CAT?
MRRRORRRW?
I know that sound.
One thing I know when I see one--
WHAP
...is a forgery.
...OH?
DUCHESS!
HOW DID YOU GET HERE?! WHY--
MRROOW!

NEXT: THERE'S A NEW ALLEYCAT IN TOWN.

CATWOMAN

VARIANT COVER GALLERY

Catwoman #45
Variant cover by Jenny Frison

Catwoman #46
Variant cover by Sozomaika

CATWOMAN #46
SWIMSUIT VARIANT COVER BY JEFF DÉKAL

CATWOMAN #47
VARIANT COVER BY SOZOMAIKA

CATWOMAN #48
VARIANT COVER BY SOZOMAIKA

CATWOMAN #49
VARIANT COVER BY SOZOMAIKA

CATWOMAN #50
VARIANT COVER BY SOZOMAIKA

CATWOMAN STUDY
BY SAMI BASRI

EIKO HASIGAWA
CATWOMAN DESIGN SKETCHES
BY NICO LEON

TOMCAT DESIGN SKETCH
BY NICO LEON